"Do you love me now?"

What answer could she possibly give? "I don't know."

Incredibly, they were still touching. Hands joined, bodies brushing lightly together.

Marriage did that, apparently. It made you so familiar with each other's bodies that you could hold each other and talk about divorce and the nonexistence of love at the same time.

"Let me prove it doesn't have to take seven minutes," he said softly.

"No…"

"Why not?" Before she could say anything, he added quickly, "No, don't answer. I know what you'll say. That if we make love, I'll think it's more proof that I've won. I don't want to prove anything."

"Then what do you want?"

A thick beat of silence, while he struggled to strip back the layers. "I just want you."

Dear Reader,

Welcome to the final book in the McKinley Medics trilogy! If I had to pick a favorite out of the three, it would be this one. Alicia and MJ are in such a different situation to that of most romance heroes and heroines, and it was both a challenge and a huge satisfaction to write their story successfully. I really hope you enjoy it.

It's such a great time to be a reader. Even just a few years ago, if you'd loved this book and were looking for more of my work, it would have been a tedious process of searching the internet, clicking through an order system and then waiting for the books to arrive in the mail, or the hit-and-miss of browsing second-hand bookstores. Let's not even talk about how we found books *before* the internet!

Now, though, when you find an author you love, much of their backlist is just a couple of mouse-clicks away, whether on the Harlequin website or elsewhere. So if you did love this book, take a look at my website, www.liliandarcy.com, where you can find out more about my backlist, and join me in celebrating the feast of books we can now read, from all our favorite authors.

Lilian

A MARRIAGE WORTH FIGHTING FOR

LILIAN DARCY

HARLEQUIN®
entertain, enrich, inspire™

Recycling programs
for this product may
not exist in your area.

ISBN-13: 978-0-373-65682-0

A MARRIAGE WORTH FIGHTING FOR

www.Harlequin.com

Printed in U.S.A.

LILIAN DARCY

has written nearly eighty books for Silhouette Romance, Special Edition and Harlequin Medical Romance. Happily married with four active children and a very patient cat, she enjoys keeping busy and could probably fill several more lifetimes with the things she likes to do—including cooking, gardening, quilting, drawing and traveling. She currently lives in Australia but travels to the United States as often as possible to visit family. Lilian loves to hear from readers. You can write to her at P.O. Box 532, Jamison P.O., Macquarie ACT 2614, Australia, or email her at lilian@liliandarcy.com.

Chapter One

Dr. Michael James McKinley Junior's life came crashing down around him at seven o'clock on a Wednesday evening in October.

Ironically, he was home considerably earlier than usual. He was feeling content. Happy, even.

Entering the lavishly lit and decorated lobby of his building, he anticipated the moment of homecoming at a level of detail that he would have been embarrassed about if anyone had known.

It would unfold something like this:

Alicia would hear his key in the door and come to meet him, giving a little cry of pleasure and surprise. He'd suggest a meal out, and she would hurry away to change and freshen her makeup and hair. The kids would still be awake. He could spend some time with them, while Alicia readied herself.

The procedure always took a while, but the results were

worth it. She was just about the most stunning woman he had ever seen. After nearly seven years of marriage he still thought so, and when he entered a social gathering with her on his arm, he felt the aura of success around both of them like a magnetic field.

So, yes, he would have to wait for Alicia to work her beauty magic, and that would be fine. He could help Nanny Maura with…well, with whatever she did with the children at this time of the evening. Their bath. Their bedtime story.

He felt he ought to know what they would be up to in their routine, but it seemed to change every few months, and it was hard to keep track of such things when he was so rarely home at an hour when they were still awake. Kids grew so fast. He had the idea Alicia had told him recently that Tyler was on the verge of giving up his daytime nap.

Or maybe he already had. MJ couldn't remember.

He took the elevator, thinking that he had better be quiet when he entered, in case Tyler was already settling into sleep. While the thought of his two-year-old son bouncing excitedly out of bed to greet him was a pleasing one in his own head, he realized that Alicia and Maura might not think of it the same way. Tyler was an exhausting little dynamo, and if he became overtired or overstimulated he was even worse.

No, he absolutely must not disrupt the sleep routine with Tyler purely for a father's selfish reasons.

At the apartment door, he registered that things were indeed pretty quiet in there. He slipped his key silently into the lock, turned the handle slowly so that it didn't make a sound and tiptoed inside.

There were no lights switched on against the gathering night, and no sounds. Still convinced that he was arriving at his children's bedtime, he crept through to the sitting room, expecting to see the night-light glowing in its socket in the hallway, or to hear the soft voices of Alicia and Maura telling Abby and Tyler good-night.

But the apartment was dark and silent. The sunset fading in the sky outside provided the only source of light, and the traffic in the canyons of the Manhattan streets below made the only sounds. No one was here. His pleasing fantasy of a warm greeting, twenty minutes of parental quality time and a relaxed evening out evaporated and left a feeling of fatigue and irritation.

He'd been at the hospital at six this morning, in surgery at six-thirty. He'd eaten lunch on the move, hadn't had a break all day, and then when he'd glimpsed the possibility of an early departure, he'd tied himself in knots to make it happen. As a reward, he could easily have accepted fellow surgeon Oliver Marks's casual suggestion of a quick drink instead of hurrying home to his family. Would it really have been too hard for Alicia to text him with a warning that she and the children might not be home? His arrival at this hour wasn't *that* rare, was it?

He checked his phone to see if he'd missed something, but, no, she really hadn't left a message. What the hell was she thinking? He didn't ask much of her in that regard, for heck's sake, and he gave her a truckload in return.

Anger rising, he went into the kitchen and flicked on a light. His gut ached with hunger, he registered, and it probably wasn't helping his mood. There'd be something in the refrigerator to hold the hunger at bay until he knew if his dinner plan with Alicia was going to come off.

He actually had his hand on the refrigerator door handle when he saw the note on the gleaming black granite countertop, pinned down by his favorite coffee mug. He swung away from the prospect of food and picked it up. *Okay, Alicia, so you* did *leave me an explanation, but why on earth didn't you text, so I could—*

It's not working, MJ. And you're never here. There's
no point saying this in person, and I doubt you'll
care. I've taken the kids to Vermont for some time
out. I'll talk to a lawyer in the next few days about
a divorce. A.

He stood with the piece of paper in his hand. His empty
stomach dropped like a stone and his temples throbbed in
shock and disbelief.

Alicia had left him.

"You see, there's green fields and little towns in Ire-
land, just like this," Nanny Maura explained to Alicia in
the same tone she might have used to explain her preference for coffee over tea. Her Irish accent was strong. "I
came to America for a taste of city life, like. I don't want
to be stuck in the country. You didn't tell me you were
gettin' a divorce when we were packin' to come up here.
I thought 'twas just for a few days."

Alicia felt a weird and close-to-hysterical desire to
laugh at the absurdity of the whole thing. Tell her nanny
she wanted a divorce before she told her husband? Good
plan! Add "Oh, by the way, I'm leaving my husband" to
her daily list of instructions about activities and errands?
No problem! Be fair to the nanny, while her life was in
tatters and her children didn't understand what was going
on? Easy peasy!

But she recognized that Maura had a point. There was
a huge difference between New York City and rural Vermont.

And maybe she didn't even need a nanny now that she
was here. It would be better, really. Maura was just another person she didn't want seeing her cry. And she'd
left her schedule of beauty treatments and shopping trips

and charity lunches behind in Manhattan. She would have plenty of time for hands-on child care.

"When would you like to leave?" Alicia asked, not sure of the answer she wanted to hear.

This had already been a painful interview, conducted once the children were safely asleep upstairs. She'd broken the truth to Maura—that there was a reason for the larger-than-usual amount of luggage they'd brought, and for the lack of the text messages to MJ that she would normally have sent if she was going up to his brother Andy's with the kids for a few days, as she'd done once or twice. *Leaving now...on the thruway.*

Maura had hidden any shock—or possibly lack of shock—behind the well-schooled facade that low-level, expendable employees learned to wear when confronted by difficult or irrational behavior from their employers. Alicia remembered the expression well from the countless times it had appeared on her own face. Maura had asked how long they would be here in Vermont, and on learning that it might be months, she'd come out with her explanation for not wanting to stay.

"When can you spare me?" Maura asked now, in response to Alicia's question.

"It doesn't matter." Because nothing much did. She'd left MJ. That was all that counted. "Whenever you want."

"Tonight?" Maura suggested hopefully. "If I check the schedule, could you drive me to the bus? A friend texted me about getting together tomorrow for—"

"Tonight is fine. I'll give you cab fare to get you to the bus station." Why go through an awkward evening? This way, Maura wouldn't even need to unpack.

"I'm sure there'd be some lovely girls up here looking for child-care work," Maura told her in an encouraging way.

"I'm sure, yes." No point in telling this girl that she didn't intend to replace her.

"You were going to give me those clothes that you didn't want anymore...." Maura offered next, referring back to a conversation from a week or two ago that Alicia had totally forgotten.

"Give me a forwarding address, as soon as you have one, and I'll mail them."

This apparently dealt with the last of Maura's concerns. Cast-off designer outfits, yippee! Her eyes lit up, and she gushed her thanks in the Irish accent that Abby and Tyler were both starting to pick up. They spent far more time with Maura than they spent with Alicia.

Well, that was about to change, big-time.

She looked at the clock.

Eight.

MJ was probably still at the hospital, or maybe winding down with a drink on the way home, with a couple of fellow doctors. When you added it up, she only saw him a few hours each week, and even those weren't spent the way she would have chosen.

He was either dog-tired and silent, wanting only to sprawl on the couch eating the tired leftovers of a meal that had been fresh two or three hours ago, or else they went out to a charity event or a gallery opening or dinner at a smart restaurant. He always touched the small of her back as they moved through one of those public spaces together, as if to say to any other man who caught his eye, "Look what I've got. Pretty special, huh?" He rarely touched her when they were alone.

It was her own fault. She hated herself for it. She'd done her best—busted her gut—to marry for money and status. She'd worked her looks and her fashion sense and her hard-won poise for all they were worth, and her strategy had succeeded.

She'd snared MJ.

She hadn't put a foot wrong.

She'd seized on that stupid, unforgettable night in Vegas when they'd gotten a little tipsy and stumbled into a garishly themed wedding chapel, and she'd gotten MJ over the line before he could sober up enough to rethink.

Brass ring, Alicia.

Married to a rich man with no prenup.

Not bad for a waitress from the wrong side of the tracks.

She'd been so goal-oriented about it that she hadn't even stopped, before the ceremony, to think whether she loved him, or whether he loved her or whether they could possibly make each other happy.

She'd done her best for almost seven years to fulfill her side of the bargain. She'd given him two children. She'd kept her looks and her figure with an almost obsessive number of gym visits and spa sessions. She'd spent his money in all the ways he wanted her to. Everything they owned, from the children's clothes to the hand-crafted dining table and matching chairs, was the product of hours of research on quality and brand names.

She'd said as little as possible about the foster homes she'd grown up in, from age ten to seventeen after Grammie died, and she'd never, ever, *ever* even hinted at the desperate straits she'd been in when he'd walked into her restaurant that first morning and given her the eye.

It wasn't going to happen. It just wasn't.

MJ's first sizzling state of shock switched quickly to anger and an absolute refusal to accept his marriage was over. He found some chicken nuggets and oven fries in the freezer and nuked them in the microwave. While they were heating, he went into the bedroom and threw a couple of days' worth of clothing into an overnight bag. The microwave pinged and he ate directly from the plastic dish, while he got on the phone and called his junior attending surgeon.

"Raj, something's come up, and I won't be available tomorrow."

"I'm sorry, Dr. McKinley. I hope nothing's wrong." The deep and slightly accented voice at the other end of the line strove to find the midpoint between professional distance and courteous concern.

"Everything's fine. Family stuff. But let me catch you up on the schedule." He switched quickly to the common language of their profession—the medical jargon and shorthand that safely took away any sense of the personal. In a couple of minutes, he covered from memory and electronic notes on his phone every patient going in for surgery tomorrow, as well as hitting the major points on several more cases that were either pre- or post-op. "Call me from the O.R. if you have any trouble with the Parker girl, because she's going to be tricky," he instructed. "You have the scans and the X-rays. But call me."

He hated delegating. He was a better surgeon than most of the orthopedic specialists he knew, and that wasn't arrogance; it was simply a fact.

Okay, correction: it was arrogance *and* fact.

He shoved the phone in his pocket, debating making another call or two—his office manager first, and then Oliver Marks, because they had a lunch plan in the works—but he could call later, or text. He wasn't texting Alicia. She'd given no warning. He'd do the same. It would be midnight or later by the time he arrived, but too bad. When your whole world turned upside down, time ceased to count.

By seven-twenty he was down in the building's underground parking garage, with his overnight bag in the trunk and his engine warming.

His marriage was *not* going to end with an arid little note from Alicia and divorce lawyers blazing their legal guns at fifty paces. He needed to confront her face-to-face, find out what was behind this, make her see.

See what?

His gut churned as he gunned the car in Reverse and squealed the tires on the echoing concrete.

See that this was impossible. Wrong. Just…impossible.

He seemed to have no other words for it than those two. Impossible and wrong. After almost five hours driving, with clenched hands aching on the wheel and jaw wired tight, he pulled into one of the twin driveways of his brother Andy's elegant and cleverly subdivided Victorian house in Radford, Vermont, with no more idea of what he wanted to say to his wife than he'd had when he started.

The hammering on the door wrenched Alicia out of her restless, unhappy sleep. For about ten seconds, her heart thumped so hard in her chest that it interfered with her breathing and her skin prickled and stung with fear, but then she knew what was happening.

MJ.

Of course.

Why hadn't she thought that he would race up here for a confrontation the moment he read her note? He had a highly developed need to win in any situation he encountered, and the prospect of a divorce was no exception.

She looked at the clock. Five minutes to midnight. It seemed appropriate. He must have gotten home from the hospital early tonight. Either that or he'd driven up here way too fast.

Probably both.

She felt sick at the thought of the imminent clash between them, and was only glad that Andy and Claudia were in New York City for a few days and weren't around to hear anything through the walls.

She had called them to ask if she and the children could use the rental apartment, "just to get away for a short break and see the fall colors," and they'd said of course she could, given her some practical instructions and told her where she could find the key. She dreaded their return four days from now, when she would have to tell them the truth.

She dreaded the next few minutes far more.

MJ hammered at the door again. Much more of it and he would wake the children, and that was the last thing she wanted. She rolled out of bed, grabbed a robe from where she'd left it on a chair in the corner of the room and hurried down, her bare feet chilling quickly on the wooden stairs and her whole body aching with reluctance and dread.

She snatched the door open just as he was about to batter his fist against it once more, so she caught him with it raised in the air, then saw the strong surgeon's fingers slowly uncurl and drop back to his side.

He hadn't showered or changed after his day's work. He was still wearing the dark suit pants and one of the crisp white business shirts he favored whenever he wasn't wearing scrubs. There was a bright moon in the sky and it picked out the white of the shirt and made it glow against the darker matte of his skin.

He'd taken off his tie and opened the shirt at the top for comfort, and his hair was windblown from driving with the car window cracked open. He liked to drive that way in all weather except the dead of winter, said it was bracing. His shirtsleeves were rolled to the elbow and the shirttail had come untucked at one side, so for once—unusually—there was something rakish about him.

His breathing was heavier than usual and ragged at the edges. His high, square brow was pleated in a tight frown, and there was an odd, numb look to his mouth, even in the low light spilling onto his face from inside the house.

He looked a mess.

He opened his mouth to speak, but then nothing came out and Alicia didn't have the words for this situation, either, so they just stared at each other, helpless and hostile and so painfully far apart.

In the end, they both spoke in the same moment.

"I'm not inviting you in."

"You can't do this, Alicia."

They went silent again. Despite what she'd just said, she almost moved aside to let him across the threshold. The patterns of seven years were hard to kick. She expected him to force the issue, simply barge past her with or without her consent, but he didn't.

He actually stepped back, spread his hands a little and conceded her victory. "All right, if you don't want me in the house, then that's your right and your choice."

"Thank you. Yes."

"But I hate that you're doing this. That you left a *note*."

"You wanted us to talk about it in front of Abby and Tyler?"

"You've taken them from their home."

"I— What was the alternative?"

"Kick me out," he said, harsh and bitter. "That's what Anna did to James."

It shocked her that he could make this reference. Anna and James had been part of their wider circle of friends until they'd divorced, after one of the most poisonous marriages Alicia had ever seen. They were still fighting mercilessly over custody of their five-year-old daughter, who was caught in the cross fire and would bear the scars.

Before Alicia could find words to protest any comparison with such a couple, MJ asked her, "Does Andy know why you're here?"

"No, not yet. He'll have to, of course, and Claudia, and everyone else."

"If you go through with the whole stupid—" he began, but he must have seen something in her face. Whatever this was on her part, it wasn't *stupid*. He didn't finish. He just stood there, a look of loss and uncertainty carved painfully deep into his even, good-looking features. When had she ever seen MJ look like that?

"I'd better go to a motel," he said.

"Why?"

"Because I'm not sleeping on my brother's front lawn. If you want me to make an appointment to talk to you in the morning, Alicia, I'll do that. Just tell me where and what time. But I'm not going back to the city until we have talked, and I think you owe me that, at least. When I saw your note—" He swallowed hard, lifted his clenched hand to his throat for a moment and didn't finish.

She saw goose bumps on his forearms. Vermont nights were getting chilly at this time of year and he wasn't dressed for it. Neither was she, with her feet bare on the hardwood of the front hall.

The idea of an "appointment" in the morning seemed worse than having him here right now. She knew she wouldn't sleep all night, and the prospect of facing down her husband at some kind of formal meeting across a café table—but who would look after the children?—made her stomach drop.

"No," she said. "Let's talk now."

"Here?" He gestured at the front porch and the yard and almost seemed willing, despite the chill and dark.

This time, she did step back. "Inside, of course."

He came across the porch and through the door, and his shirtsleeve would have brushed the front of her robe if she hadn't leaned a crucial inch closer to the hallway wall. "Where's Maura? I don't want her—"

"She left."

"Left?"

"Quit. She didn't want to be in Vermont. Too rural. I gave her money for a cab and a bus ticket back to the city. You probably crossed paths with her somewhere near Albany."

She closed the heavy wooden door and followed him toward the front living room, but he turned suddenly while they were still in the hall and pulled her into his arms, with a disturbing mix of authority and hesitation. "Don't— don't do this."

"What?"

His muscles were hard around her, all knotted and demanding. "Any of it! This gesture. We have two children. A partnership."

"It's not a gesture."

"Forgive me if I get the semantics wrong," he almost yelled.

"You're right. There's so much else wrong. Semantics is not even the tip of the iceberg."

"What else is wrong?"

"Everything, MJ. What's right? Tell me one thing that's right about our marriage?" She pushed at his arms. They were so rigid they were almost painful, and she had no desire whatsoever to soften into them when they were like that.

But then she caught the drift of scent from his skin, a

mix of soap and nuttiness, and for a moment it made her crumble inside. The scent of safety, she'd thought when it first became familiar to her, seven years ago. A precious, desperately valued scent that said everything was going to be okay now. She didn't need to be scared anymore. She didn't need to be alone.

It was such a powerful memory. It almost undermined her resolve. Unconsciously, she relaxed a little and felt his hold on her grow closer, but at the same time softer, a little less like a vise. His hands slipped down the back of her robe, warming her spine, coming to rest in the inward curve of her waist.

He laced his fingers together, leaned back a little and looked at her, eyes raking over her as if taking inventory or examining a precious possession in search of flaws. Hell, he couldn't possibly think he'd won this already, could he?

She'd *left* him, left her marriage, and it wasn't a mere gesture. She meant it. She was serious.

And yet, why shouldn't he think he'd won? He won so many things, so often. Discussions about where and when to go for their vacation, inevitably choosing status destinations that they could talk about with their friends. The decision about building his medical career in New York City, following his father's and grandfather's tradition. She hadn't even dared to suggest that somewhere else might be a worthwhile choice. The debate about when they should start trying for a baby, when Alicia would have preferred to wait another year or two—and then of course she had gotten pregnant the first month.

But if Alicia thought she was winning this one, why wasn't she pushing him away? she wondered. She should be!

"You have a beautiful apartment," he said, still angry

but softer about it. "You have a platinum credit card. I buy you gifts. I take you out. When do I ever say no to any of it? Your personal trainer, your wardrobe, the help we pay top dollar for."

There.

Right there.

That was the whole problem.

In a nutshell.

She was bitterly unsurprised that he'd come out with such a catalog of material benefits, too. Of course it was the first thing he would think of, and the fault lay as much at her own door as at his. More so. The only thing that surprised her—*always* surprised her, in a guilty, self-doubting way—was that he seemed satisfied with his side of the bargain. What did he get out of the arrangement? There must have been hundreds of women who would have been worth more to him and who would have married him for better reasons.

This was the thing that made it impossible for her to continue their marriage.

He thought she'd married him for what he could give her. The money. The status. The pampered lifestyle. And for whatever reason, he was content with that.

Worse, when she searched her heart and searched her memories, she couldn't find the proof to tell him he was wrong. She'd been too desperate at the time to even think about love or the deeper levels of a partnership.

She wrenched herself out of his arms, sick with shame and disappointment at herself and at him. Of course their marriage had failed. How could either of them expect any other outcome, given its flawed foundations?

"Go back to New York, MJ," she said on a harsh whisper, while she wondered if she was a different person from that terrified twenty-three-year-old seven years ago, or if she would soon discover that she hadn't changed at all.

Chapter Two

Seven years earlier...

"Mail," Alicia's boss said shortly, tossing her a handful of envelopes, which made her heart sink as soon as she saw them. "Came yesterday."

The last time she'd moved apartments, she'd won Tony Cottini's permission to use his restaurant address for her mail delivery, since her job seemed a more stable entity than her place of residence, but she regretted it every time these letters came.

It was so obvious what they were. Overdue account notices, containing increasingly strident demands for payment. They were cold things, echoing the cold of the November day outside.

"Thanks," she told him quickly, then stuffed the mail in the battered purse hanging on a hook in a dingy alcove and hurried to the serving window in front of the kitchen to line four plates of hot food along her arm.

Tony wasn't a bad boss—if he had been, maybe she wouldn't have fallen into her current trap with the mailing address, because she wouldn't have dared to ask—but he still had a healthy interest in her attaining maximum productivity levels at all times.

She delivered the food with a smile, took the order from the next table and skimmed back to the kitchen to slap it in front of the short-order cook, calling it out as she did so. "Three specials, two eggs over easy with bacon and hash browns, one on whole wheat, one scrambled, sausage and home fries, white toast."

Okay, now Table Three.

It was only seven in the morning. Her feet had already begun to ache, but that would taper off after the rush hit its peak at around eleven. By the time she finished her double shift twelve hours after that, the rest of her would be so tired that the old reliable feet almost wouldn't care.

Table Three had a doctor at it, eating by himself. She could tell he was a doctor because a) the restaurant was only a block from a major Manhattan hospital, so doctors grabbed a quick meal here quite often, b) he was reading a gigantic medical textbook and c) he'd forgotten to take off his name badge, which read Dr. Michael McKinley, Jr.

"What can I get you?" she asked him, coffeepot in hand.

At Tony's, they didn't bother with all that hi-my-name's-Alicia-and-I'll-be-your-server-today stuff. Again, he was a decent boss that way. He just growled at them every now and then, "Say whatever greeting you like to the customer. Just be sincere and say it with a smile."

Oops, she'd forgotten the smile.

She put it on.

The one she'd practiced.

The one she'd *paid* for.

Or rather, borrowed the money for, at the kind of horrible interest rate you had no choice about when you had an unimpressive credit history.

The one she was, in other words, *still* paying for.

Dr. Michael McKinley Junior looked up from the giant book in response to her question, and his gaze arrived at her face in time to see the smile—its dutiful dawning, its practiced beauty and its slow fade when she thought about how much she still owed for these perfect straight white teeth.

He ordered the biggest breakfast on the menu and held out his cup for coffee like a thirsty man in the desert, which made her think he'd probably been working all night. She filled it neatly, to the perfect height.

There was a pride in doing good work. She'd learned that as an actress—okay, wannabe actress—and she'd always tried to carry it through into the rest of her life. Look at it this way: What if she had to play a waitress in a major movie someday? What if she was chosen to front a lifestyle TV show? Or feature in a national ad campaign for a top-selling brand of coffee? Or if a modeling photo shoot called for her to pose with a steaming cup in her hand?

Those fantasies didn't come very often anymore. They'd been scoured away by six years of struggling to survive in Manhattan, since she'd arrived here off a bus from Tennessee at the age of seventeen. Six years of fitting acting classes and auditions around restaurant shifts. Six years of scraping together the money to eat and sleep, as well as updating her modeling portfolio and fixing her damned teeth.

She'd been told to do this by several modeling agencies, and it had seemed like an investment in her future, the one key piece of the puzzle that was missing. Once she had straight white teeth, the work would start to flow and the money would pour in.

But it still wasn't happening, and there was this horrible slippery slope where you paid off the loan for the teeth with a credit card and then got another credit card to cover the maxed-out balance on the first one, and it was *so hard* to get ahead.

When did something stop being an investment and start being money poured down the drain? She hadn't taken any of those expensive acting and voice and movement classes for a while, and her photo portfolio was more than three years old.

"You're a beautiful girl," she'd been told a thousand times. "But…"

Fill in the blank.

You're two inches too short. You're too big in the bust. You don't have the voice. You're too small in the bust. You don't have the dance training. You're a model and we're looking for an actress. You're an actress and we're looking for someone who can sing…who can speak French… who can ride a unicycle…who can dance with bears while wrapping a flaming cobra around her neck and juggling ten chain saws.

Yeah, and don't even go near the X-rated ways to complete the "someone who can" equation. This was one of her few sources of pride. She'd never stooped to porn videos or the casting couch.

But she was *scared* sometimes. Scared every day. She had nothing to fall back on. No close family, since Grammie's death. Some distant cousins she didn't even know. Friends in only a little less bad shape than she was. She could never call on them to bail her out. Most of them, she didn't even know if they really were friends. More like fellow prisoners in the same trap. Maybe every single one of them would scramble over her dead body if it gave them a route to success. How much scrambling would she be prepared to do herself?

The desperate plans went around and around in her head. Work more double shifts so she could pay off the debt and get some money saved. Abandon her dreams of success, leave the city and find somewhere cheaper to live, take some night courses to earn a more realistic qualification.

She had nothing in that area, because she'd been so sure that the "You're so beautiful" she'd heard since the age of nine would be enough.

There it was, right now, on Dr. Michael McKinley Junior's face. *You're so beautiful.* He didn't say it out loud, but she'd learned to read it even when it wasn't spoken. It was like the twenty-seven supposed Eskimo words for *snow,* so many variants of the same thing.

You're so beautiful, but you're out of my league.

You're so beautiful, but you're not my type.

You're so beautiful, and I'm such a sleaze I'm not going to even hide than I'm looking down your uniform blouse.

In Dr. McKinley's case, it seemed to be more like "You're so beautiful, wow, you're actually distracting me from my coffee," and he looked so exhausted and bowled over and unaware of his own reaction that it was quite cute, because he was a good-looking man himself. Aged around thirty, she thought, with an imposing height and build, darkly even features and a warm, well-shaped mouth. So it was no hardship to meet his eye and lift the wattage of the smile a notch or two higher.

She gave him his breakfast *perfectly.*

And then he went, and that was that.

Or not.

Because he appeared again for supper just before she

clocked off for the night, and he remembered her and told her, "You work longer hours than I do."

"But your work is more important," she answered, which was from-the-heart to a stupid extent, considering Dr. McKinley's casual comment.

She had a complex, sentimental feeling about doctors, dating from Grammie's illness, when a couple of them had been so good and thoughtful and kind, and yet they hadn't been able to make Grammie better. That was thirteen years ago now, when she was ten, but it still colored her reactions sometimes. Colored her life always.

"Thank you," Dr. McKinley said. "It's nice to hear that."

And she could tell he had a healthy ego, but there was a sincerity to the words all the same, and the *you're-so-beautiful* in his eyes had an extra something to it, a little spark.

And suddenly, right there while she poured his coffee, some instinct told her she needed to nurture and fan that spark more carefully and strategically and hardheadedly than she'd ever nurtured anything in her life.

Because maybe, just maybe, there might be something in it for her.

Chapter Three

She meant it, MJ could tell.

Go back to New York.

Even though Alicia had only whispered the words, they had more force for him than if she'd yelled them and physically pushed him toward the door.

She never fought him. On anything. It drove him crazy sometimes. He wanted to tell her, "I'm not asking for that from you. I don't need such perfect agreement and acquiescence with everything I say and everything I want. That's not why I married you. You are allowed to be a person, Alicia. An independent person, not just my wife. Your total obedience was never part of the bargain."

So why didn't he say it?

Standing here right now, in the hallway of the rental apartment attached to his younger brother's house, looking at his beautiful blonde wife, the question reared up at him like a snake and made him paralyzed.

Why didn't he ever say it?

Because he was scared, he realized. He was bloody terrified that if he pulled their marital bargain out into the bright light of day—or rather the bright light of *words*—the things they said to each other would shatter any possibility of keeping the life they had.

The life he wanted.

Really, MJ?

Hell, yes, he wanted what he had! Stellar career, beautiful, capable wife, happy children, well-organized home life.

Which brought him back to square one. Out of the blue, Alicia wanted a divorce and was standing in his brother's hallway in Vermont, telling him to leave.

I'm exhausted.

Another inconvenient and powerful realization. She wanted him to go, and he was tempted to do just that—fling himself angrily out of here and tear back down the highway he'd just driven. But he didn't think he would be safe on the road for another five-hour stint. He probably hadn't been particularly safe driving up.

"I'll check in to a motel," he told her for the second time tonight.

"Will you find one, at this hour?"

"That's not your concern, is it?" The words were sour and harsh with anger, and he saw her flinch.

"MJ—"

"There'll be something. I won't have to go beyond Albany. I can drive that far, without going off the road."

She said nothing to this, and he thought it was because they had no precedents to go on. They'd never argued. There was never anything to argue about. She did what he wanted, said what he wanted, kept quiet.

Didn't see him all that much.

Didn't see enough of him for the two of them to rub against each other the way a married couple usually did.

That was one of the things she'd said in her note, which he discovered he already knew by heart. *You're never here.* What did she want with that? He was one of the most successful orthopedic specialists in Manhattan. The kind that A-list celebrities came to after a skiing accident or when their kid broke an arm in the playground. The kind who put together seriously broken bodies flown in from a radius of hundreds of miles, or fixed limbs made hopelessly dysfunctional through trauma or genetic accident. He worked ninety hours a week.

And she benefited from those ninety hours with every breath she took. The beauty treatments, the shopping trips, the time for charity work that was far more about being seen at $3,000-a-plate fundraiser dinners than it was about the Amazon rain forest or the tigers in Bengal.

He suddenly came upon a bitter place inside himself where crouched this ugly little belief that she *liked* seeing so little of him. Shoot, it hurt to think that, but he realized he'd thought it for a while.

Thought it but never allowed the thought any space, kept the ugly little thing in a small, murky cave deep inside himself and was too busy and too in-demand as a surgeon to remember it was there, most of the time.

Now it knifed through him with a sharp awareness that almost made him gasp out loud. He controlled himself with the same iron will that helped him survive round-the-clock stints of surgery, and told her, "We both need some time. This has hit me from left field, Alicia."

"Yes," she replied briefly, as if she wasn't surprised.

"Maybe it shouldn't have. Maybe you'll say that's a huge part of the problem. That I didn't see it coming. That I didn't—"

Hell, he couldn't go on. He was going to break down if he did. The degree of his emotion appalled him. And her blank, distant reaction appalled him more. She was just standing there, as if she was made of marble. As pale as marble, too, almost. But if this was painful to her, it wasn't the same kind of pain he felt himself.

"I'm sorry." The words were wrenched out of him as if a mystical hand had just reached inside his throat and pulled. He didn't know what he was apologizing for, and he didn't wait to see how she would react, just tore out through the front door, across the porch and down the steps to the car, where the engine still ticked as it cooled in the chilly night.

He knew he'd be back, and soon, but he didn't know what he would say or do when he came.

Alicia felt shaky and sick as she heard the car drive away into the silent dark of the sleeping street. She'd expected to feel angry.

Oh, it was so strange!

She'd been so completely unsurprised to find him banging on that front door, demanding entrance in the middle of the night, but everything after that hadn't gone the way she'd thought it would at all.

At some level, she'd *wanted* all the ego and impatience and one-sided demands. MJ so rarely betrayed any sense of vulnerability. Just those tiny glimpses in his last few words tonight had rocked her and undermined her certainty far more than he could have done with undiluted anger.

And then he'd *listened* to her.

She'd asked him to go, and he'd done so, and now she was left knowing she wouldn't sleep tonight. He had talked about the two of them needing time. Writing that note to him this morning, she would have said that time was the last thing she needed. She'd had a ton of that.

She'd been thinking for months about leaving him. Flirting with the idea at first. *What if I just took the children and left?* Not meaning it, just playing with it. But then the thoughts had grown more serious, the plans more detailed.

She would have to leave the city, she'd decided, so that there was some physical distance between the two of them and so that neither of them had to face pressure from his father.

Who would hate this, she knew, because he expected perfection and order from his children.

She would have to soften the reality for Abby and Tyler, and leaving the city would help, there, too. They were so small; she didn't want them to witness the ugliness and conflict. She had to find a secure, happy environment for them from the beginning, even if there was a later transition to a different, permanent home. Andy's rental apartment checked all the boxes.

When she'd reached a concrete decision, there hadn't been any momentous last straw to make it happen; it was simply a long, gradual accumulation, with a handful of moments that stood out from the rest.

Like the night Andy and Claudia had announced their engagement and their plans for the small, informal wedding that would be taking place in New York City just a couple of weeks from now. Alicia had urged Claudia to go for something bigger, even if it meant waiting, and when she thought back, she realized that MJ's sister, Scarlett, had probably interpreted that in the worst way.

Alicia knew that at least some members of the McKinley family believed she'd married MJ for his money and status.

Well, they were right, weren't they?

It was stupid and pointless to regret the rush of their Las Vegas wedding. Would their marriage have been any healthier and happier if they'd started it off with a well-organized splash, months in the planning? Would it have happened at all?

Doubtful.

MJ would have been bound to see sense and realize he could do so much better.

She shivered. It really was cold in the house. She'd tried the heating earlier tonight, but nothing happened when she touched the controls on the electronic thermostat. Apparently Andy hadn't yet turned on the furnace, although he hadn't mentioned it during their short phone call. Maybe he shared MJ's preference for bracing doses of fresh air at a temperature of fifty degrees or less.

She crept upstairs and back to bed, but her churning feelings, her blank sense of the future and her freezing feet wouldn't let her sleep, and when Abby and Tyler came bouncing into the room at just after six-thirty, she wasn't sure how she was going to get through the day.

MJ checked out of the cheap motel on the outskirts of Albany at seven in the morning. His colleagues would be surprised to see him in surgery at eleven-thirty, after what he'd said to Raj on the phone last night, but it wasn't their business.

Later, at his office, he would have to grab Carla, his office manager, and go through his schedule with her. He had to be realistic. If he and Alicia were going to give themselves a chance, then *he* needed to give them time. Time to talk. Time to compromise. Time to mine down to the depths of what was wrong.

It hit him again as he drove.

He did *not* want a divorce.

His throat hurt over it. His whole body hurt, knotted with the tension of rebellion and pain and refusal to accept his marriage was over.

He was not getting a divorce. He didn't damn well believe in it! Not when you had kids. Not when you had a partnership that should have worked.

He accepted that Alicia wasn't doing this on a shallow whim, and so he was going to have to work at changing her mind, and if she wasn't expecting a fight from him over this, then she didn't know him very well.

Did she know him well?

The question struck him suddenly, as if he had a passenger sitting beside him, grilling him on the issue.

Did he know her?

Well, of course they knew each other! They each knew what the other ate for breakfast. They knew the sounds each other made in bed. He knew she liked diamonds and sapphires but not emeralds. She knew he detested reality TV.

Did any of that count as real knowledge?

They'd rushed into their marriage. He recognized that. He'd even recognized it at the time. He hadn't thought it mattered, because in the moment he'd felt so incredibly, exhilaratingly sure. He'd had this all-seeing, all-knowing confidence—arrogance, let's face it—that he could see the whole picture and that he understood what would make their marriage work better than anyone else.

How wrong had he been?

Chapter Four

Seven years earlier...

"Want to dress up tonight?"

Alicia gave MJ a questioning look and tucked the fluffy white hotel towel a little tighter between her breasts, and he thought that the gesture was an unconscious betrayal.

Of her increasingly urgent inner questions about where this relationship was going. Of the fact that the variety in her wardrobe was getting thin.

"I want to go someplace really special," he added, so that she'd know he had plans.

"I'd love that," she said, then warned him with a slow and almost cheeky smile. "But you've seen the dress before."

"That's okay. Gives me confidence. You've never yet worn anything I didn't like."

He suspected that most of her wardrobe came from

charity stores, because even he, with no interest in fashion, could see that her carefully put-together outfits weren't at the forefront of style. But she wore them with the aura of an Oscar-winning actress on the red carpet, as if she knew that she looked stunning, and as if she was wearing fifteen thousand dollars worth of fabric and design on her upper body alone.

He admired the bravado of the performance, and that she was successful at it. She was an astute shopper, and you had to really look closely to see that she wasn't wearing a designer label after all, or that if it was, it was "vintage," aka secondhand, rather than new.

Few people, male or female, did look that closely. They were too busy being struck dumb by her lush bow of a mouth, her dazzling blue eyes, her dynamite figure and her perfect bone structure.

With the towel still carefully wrapped around her, she walked across the carpet to the mirror-fronted closet that ran along one side of the narrow entrance to their hotel room, and he couldn't take his eyes from her prettily manicured bare feet, which appeared to react with a sensual delight to the lush thickness, as if they were more accustomed to walking on nails.

This was rapidly becoming one of MJ's favorite leisure-time activities—lying on a king-size bed surrounded by a heap of snowy pillows while he watched Alicia dress. The hair and makeup routines he could skip. Those took place in the secrecy of the bathroom, they were too arcane and technical, and the blow dryer was noisy. In any case, he considered that she looked just as good with no makeup, bed hair and a pillow-crease mark across her cheek.

But the way she shimmied her breasts into a push-up lace bra, or let a sheath of silky fabric slide down her body…

In the month since they'd started sleeping together, Alicia getting dressed was a process that frequently reversed itself before it was even finished and transformed into a completely different activity in a very satisfactory way.

Not today.

Today she was a little coy.

She did that sometimes—went inexplicably distant as if she didn't want him to have too much of a good thing. When he reached out his arms for her—now, for example—she did that smile again and shook her head. "Later."

"Why?" he lazily asked.

"Because later I'll taste of chocolate."

He didn't point out that they could have now as well as later. He thought he understood why she needed to keep a hold of the reins in their relationship sometimes, and it didn't bother him.

Tonight, especially, he'd been quite sincere in what he'd told her. He did want this to be a really special, unforgettable evening. He'd bought her something. His anticipation about seeing her face when she opened the gift almost outweighed his anticipation about her tasting of chocolate.

Forty-five minutes later, she was ready to go, wearing a splashy, strappy floral dress that showed off the light golden glow of her newly tanned shoulders. She'd spent most of the afternoon out by the pool, catching the March sunshine that was so much stronger here than it would have been in New York, while he'd gone off on his covert shopping mission.

While she was in the bathroom just now, he'd slipped the gift into the inside pocket of his suit jacket and he hoped the bulge didn't show. He didn't want to give it to her yet. Before dessert, maybe, when they were both replete with good food and just pleasantly mellow from a glass or two of wine.

He curved his arm around her bare shoulders as they walked into the five-star restaurant together. Her shoulders were sun-warmed and touched with pink and perfectly smooth. He wanted to pull her close, but this was a public place and he hadn't been raised to feel comfortable about full-on displays of affection in front of strangers. Instead, he let his hand slide down to the small of her back and recognized his own sense of proud possession.

She turns every head in the room, and she's with me.

He was dizzy about it. Even dizzier an hour and a half into their meal, after a little more wine than he'd planned.

"I'm having a great time," he told her.

"Me, too." She smiled. "You can be pretty funny, do you know that?"

"So can you."

He'd never felt like this before. An ambitious young doctor didn't have much time to devote to finding the right woman. Of course he'd dated. During his internship, three years ago, he'd been quite serious about a fellow doctor whom he'd met on his rotation through the E.R.

But it had been a nightmare, in the end. Adrienne was a single mother. She did a really great job with it but juggled the most horrific schedule. The deeper he went into the relationship, the more it appalled him. They went weeks without spending any kind of quality time together, and he wasn't comfortable in the role of instant dad. As the eldest son in the McKinley family, he shared his father's perception that they were building a dynasty, and he wanted kids of his own.

If Adrienne hadn't had her own mother close at hand, she couldn't possibly have managed motherhood and the demands of medical study, but it meant that MJ felt as if he was taking her mom on board as well as her son. Cynthia was a nice woman, but the countless hours of help she gave her daughter made her feel entitled to comment and judge and interfere at will about everything. He couldn't blame her for that, but it didn't mean he liked it.

To cut a long story short, the relationship hadn't worked, and he'd come away from it after six months feeling as if there just wasn't room for both people in a partnership to have such a full schedule and so many emotional demands.

He'd made a conscious decision at that point only to get involved with women who had a little less ambition and drive, and preferably not much baggage. A relationship shouldn't be harder and more demanding than his career, for heck's sake. A relationship was about downtime and emotional nourishment.

He'd only known Alicia for four months and wasn't yet asking himself any questions about the future, but so far she gave him more emotional nourishment than any woman he'd ever met.

Just that smile…

"Dessert menu?" she asked.

"Wait a moment. I have something." He reached into his pocket and pulled out the square, dark blue velvet box.

She saw it in his hand, went completely still as if in shock, put her fingertips against her mouth and swallowed. "Oh, MJ…" she breathed.

"Open it," he said softly and passed it to her. She couldn't take her eyes off it, and cradled it in her hand as if it was as fragile as a quail's egg.

"Yes," she said, half-laughing, almost in tears. "Oh, yes!"

Her fingers were shaking. It took her a good thirty seconds to get the box open, and there it was, the diamond hair clip dazzling white and gold against the deep blue. He'd had a private, hour-long session in the back room of the very exclusive Vegas jewelry store this afternoon, where he'd been shown tray after tray of bracelets, necklaces and earrings, but this was what he'd settled on because of her beautiful hair.

"Ohh," she said abruptly and put the box down. "Oh, wow. Wow. It's—it's beautiful."

"Do you like it?" Rather an ego-driven question, he realized at once. But it was sincere, too. He wanted to know. He wanted her to love it. "They're diamonds."

In case she was in any doubt.

Six figures' worth. He wasn't going to reveal the exact price he'd paid, but she would have to realize it was a lot.

She was staring down at it, hadn't moved to touch it again, wasn't speaking. He took a too-large gulp of wine and regretted it. He already felt a little hazy. Focusing on her face more closely, he realized she wasn't reacting quite the way he'd expected.

"I—I can't accept this, MJ."

"Of course you can. Why not?"

She groped for words, while the velvet box sat on the table in front of her, untouched. Why didn't she take out the clip and look at it more closely? Trace those pretty fingertips over the diamonds and gold? Why was she having such trouble? He could almost see the wheels turning in her head.

Stupidly, he took yet another gulp of wine, and then he looked at the square velvet box again and suddenly he knew. She had thought there was going to be a ring in there. She was convinced. It was the right shape, maybe a tiny bit larger, such an easy mistake to make. What had she said to him before she'd opened it?

"Yes. Oh, yes!"

Ah, hell, and there *should* have been a ring.

In an instant, it was startlingly clear to him. She'd thought at first that he was proposing, but she'd quickly realized her mistake. Anything less than a ring looked to her like a payment for sex, like the beginning of the end. She was a waitress. It was probably what she thought she deserved.

Now she was trying to calculate whether the gift was worth—*literally* worth—taking, whether it was all she was ever going to get from the relationship, whether he was using it to start the process of kissing her off and what room she had to maneuver in all of this.

It made him wince and it made him ache.

He'd wanted so much to make her happy with the expensive gift, not send her into a spin of desperate calculation and doubt like this. He cared about her happiness, he realized. Cared far more than he'd thought.

"Let's get married." He said it before he knew he was going to, and it was crazy and impulsive and the exact opposite of his usual considered decision-making, but he didn't want to take it back. He took her hands across the table. "Alicia, it's not a ring. You thought it was going to be, but it's not and that's my fault, but let's get married anyhow, and we'll get a ring for you later."

She laughed, not daring to believe him now, when she'd been wrong before. "Married, MJ?"

"Yes, why the hell not? Tonight. This is Vegas. If we skip dessert, we can probably be married in half an hour."

"Half an hour? Married?"

"I want to, Alicia. I really, really want to!"

Now she was laughing and crying. The tears sparkled on her lashes, and he didn't regret what he'd said for a moment. "Yes, MJ. If you really mean it, yes!" she said.

It took a little longer than half an hour but not by much. At ten in the evening, there they were in the glitzy chapel, wearing their dinner clothes, still pleasantly mellow and happy from the wine, and saying their sketchy vows.

Alicia wore her strapless dress, a kiss of sunburn on her shoulders, and the glittering diamond barrette in her gorgeous piled-up hair, while MJ's whole body buzzed with a giddy sense of triumph and rightness that almost took his breath away.

Chapter Five

But that was then.

He arrived home from the hospital at nine o'clock. It was now twenty-six hours, 520 miles of driving, four hours of surgery and five hours of medical admin and patient care since he'd first found Alicia's note.

The kitchen was just the way he'd left it, with the microwave dish still sitting on the countertop, containing some crumbs and half a shriveled chicken nugget. It was, what, Thursday? Their housekeeper, Rosanna, came on Mondays and Fridays. She usually replenished their grocery supplies on a Friday, he understood, so there was probably not much food left in the place.

He'd never needed to think about this kind of thing in his life. Mom was a great cook. In college and medical school, he had the full meal plan. Later, living on his own, he'd eaten out or ordered in for almost every meal that he hadn't grabbed at the hospital café. On his marriage, he'd given Alicia a free hand and she'd set everything up. Most of the time, he never even knew where it came from—if Rosanna had cooked it, or Alicia herself, or if it came from a deli or a caterer. This was New York City. Food just…was.

Except when it wasn't.

His gut felt terrible, a mix of physical hunger and emotional wrenching that he didn't know how to damp down. He didn't want to go out. He didn't want to hunt up takeout menus and get on the phone. He didn't really want to eat at all but knew he should.

Life went on.

He needed to have some semblance of a brain in place, in order to talk to Alicia about what happened next.

In the end, he found a couple of eggs and a loaf of sliced bread in the freezer, and made an inept version of scrambled eggs on toast. He didn't think to put butter in the skillet, so the eggs stuck, and when he tried adding water to unstick them, he ended up with unappetizing eggy slush ladled onto toast that went soggy in seconds.

He ate it anyhow, disguised with some chunks of cheese and a too-liberal shake of pepper and salt.

Then he called his wife.

She would know it was him before she even had the phone to her ear. *MJ* would have come up on her phone screen. And she must have expected a call from him, anyhow. She knew he wasn't going to let this go. She sounded guarded and polite, and he fought for the right tone.

"How're the kids?" he heard himself ask. Heard the scratch in his voice, too.

Hell, it hurt not to be with them. Alicia would have said he barely saw them, but, shoot, that didn't mean he didn't care. His awareness of their peacefully sleeping presence when he came home to the apartment at night or left in the early morning nourished him at a level he'd never tried to put into words. The times he did see them were incredibly precious, if demanding, and for all the times when he wasn't around, he had enormous confidence in Alicia as a mother.

Damn, did he not tell her that enough, or something?

He tried to remember the last time he had, and couldn't. To him it was so obvious—why did she need to hear it?

"They're asleep," she said. "Tired."

"What did you do today?"

"Went to a park. We had a picnic. Which ended up taking place in the car because it began to rain. But we had fun anyway." The forced cheeriness in the word *fun* reminded him that he wasn't the only one who'd had to carry on as usual today, despite the upheaval of their separation.

"I'm glad," he answered her mechanically, then cut to the chase. "What have you said to them, Alicia? What do they know?"

"I haven't said anything yet. For them, we're on vacation, that's all. At some point, of course—"

He jumped in. "You can't just spring it on them. And you can't do it when I'm not around. We have to tell them together. I will not have my children exposed to that kind of conflict or have them doubt my role as their father in any way." In his urgency, he spoke with more anger than he'd intended.

Hell, he was so unused to anything like this!

He wasn't thinking of the prospect of divorce, there— of course he wasn't used to that!

But he wasn't accustomed in *any* area to having his will thwarted. This seemed almost shameful on his part, certainly nothing to be proud of, but that's how it was. He was a top surgeon. People did what he wanted. Always.

Alicia, too. Maura and their previous nanny, Kate, another two nannies before that. And Rosanna, the rare times he saw her.

Abby and Tyler were almost the only human beings who ever defied him.

"Time to get out of the bath now, sweetheart. Both of you."

"No! Not yet!"

"No, no, no!"

He realized he wasn't comfortable when that happened. He tended to opt out and have Alicia or the nanny take over. *"Here, they're unmanageable tonight, and I'm tired."*

But Alicia was speaking now. He focused quickly on her voice down the line. "Of course I won't just spring it on them, MJ. Is that really who you think I am? Someone who would risk destroying my own children's sense of emotional security that way, like Anna and James are doing? Someone who would use them as a weapon against you?"

"No... No, I'm not suggesting that."

"You seemed to be."

"Look, it wasn't intentional. It wasn't. Our marriage is nothing like what Anna and James had. If you're saying it is—"

"No, no, I'm not. You're right. There's no comparison."

Something they agreed on! He felt a brief moment of relief.

"All I'm saying is that I want us to do this right. If we have to do it at all. I don't want it, Alicia. If there's anything I can do, anything I can say, any way I can change, or we can both change, *talk* so that—" He stopped.

Hell, was he *begging*?

She stayed silent at the end of the phone, after he'd broken off. He waited, head pounding, jaw tight. Should he seize the window opened up by her silence? Take the initiative? He didn't know how.

She spoke again before he had any answers. "You'll have to come up here again." The words were slow and careful. "I do know that. Maybe it's best not to put it off. Can you get some time?"

"This weekend," he said quickly, while the back of his mind buzzed, rearranging his schedule, working out a few favors he could call in. In his position, it wasn't easy to get a chunk of time off at short notice.

Alicia knew that, and he hoped she would see his willingness as a step toward—

Toward having this whole thing just go away!

But he'd begun to accept that this wasn't going to be an easy fix.

"If you could, that would be great," Alicia said, still with that slow, careful way of talking, as if she was having to bite her tongue not to yell at him or blurt out a hundred deeply felt grievances. "It doesn't need to be the whole weekend...."

"It's going to be the whole weekend. I'll drive up Saturday morning, back down Sunday night." Another ten hours in the car. He didn't care.

"All right, if you want. I think you'd better book into a motel."

"What will the children think of that?"

Thick silence. "Make a reservation, please, MJ. It—it may turn out that you can cancel it..."

He felt a rush of relief and hope.

Short-lived.

"...if we can stay civilized enough for you to sleep in the study."

"In the study?"

"I made up a folding bed there for Maura—of course, she never used it—and I haven't put it away yet. There are really only the two bedrooms. Abby and Tyler are sharing. But they don't need to know where you're sleeping. Anyway, they're not going to see our choice of sleeping arrangements—" a pause "—the way an adult sees it."

"No."

So this was how she saw the physical side of their marriage, as a "choice of sleeping arrangements." It felt like a body blow. Like a kick in the—

Yeah. There.

"Was there anything else you wanted to say?" Alicia asked him carefully.

"Uh, no. Face-to-face, of course. But not now. Could you call and cancel Rosanna for tomorrow? I don't want her—"

"Yes, okay, that's probably a good idea." She took a breath. "So can you text me with a rough arrival time? In case I'm out with the kids?"

"Sure." He got through another couple of rounds of practical back-and-forth, then flipped the phone into the breast pocket of his shirt, his mind still snagged on the "sleeping arrangements" thing like ripped skin snagged on a rusty nail.

In other words, it hurt. Bad.

Did she mean it that way? Was she completely dismissing the sex life he'd always viewed with such satisfaction and pleasure and pride?

They were great in bed together. They were. They were dynamite.

But even as he thought this, he realized his attitude was a little out-of-date. He was thinking back to that sizzling week in Las Vegas and the vacations they'd taken together early in their marriage, before they'd decided to try for a baby. Those times stood out in his memory like a series of magazine-perfect honeymoons, four or five of them, some only a couple of days, others a week or more. Las Vegas, Bermuda, Paris, Aspen, Martinique.

He could call up a thousand pictures. Alicia in a red bikini with her luscious breasts bouncing as she walked along a tropical beach and her blond hair shining brightly in the sun. Himself taking the bikini off in the privacy of their suite, by pulling at that saucy string bow that only just held things together in the front. Lying back in a foaming private spa together, champagne within reach. Sitting across the softly lit table from her at a three-star restaurant, anticipating the moment when they would get back to their Paris hotel room and he could pull her into his arms.

At home, lately, sex had been different, he realized. They were both tired. He needed the release but didn't need the slow, sensual build. It was over in minutes, and even though he was vaguely aware that she didn't show the abandonment she once had, he put this down to the same priorities that dampened his own performance—just do it and get some sleep.

While he was burning with the knowledge that he would miss her body in his bed the way he would have missed air or gravity, she seemed to be implying that she wouldn't miss their lovemaking at all. For the first time, it occurred to him that maybe she'd left him for the worst and hardest reason of all.

She'd found another man.

At the very thought, he felt as if someone had knifed him in the gut.

When he dragged himself into bed at ten o'clock, he felt her absence like an illness, and when he woke up at three after a couple of hours of unrestful sleep, he found he was holding her pillow in his arms as if he was cradling his own pain.

It smelled of her hair and her shampoo…it just smelled

of *her*...and he was surprised that she'd left it behind now that he thought about it. Very surprised. She almost always took it with her when they went away, cramming it into a suitcase or nestling it into the corner of the backseat in the car. Its presence in their marital bed spoke to him, helped him, even though he couldn't work out what it said.

He almost slid the pillow back to its rightful position on her side of the bed, but then in a moment of...he didn't know—weakness? hope?—he pulled it closer again and hugged it like a child, or like an ardent lover, until sleep came over him.

Chapter Six

"What's happening today, Mommy?" Abby wanted to know, five minutes after she woke up.

"Well, we need to go to the store. And I thought we might check out the library. Then we'll come home and make cookies, hey?"

"Cookies!" Tyler said.

"Won't that be fun?" Alicia agreed brightly.

It would. And also a nightmare. Faking having fun with your kids was harder than faking an orgasm, and, yes, Alicia had done both.

Like a good wife and mother, she felt guilty about both, also.

But, oh, yesterday had been so hard!

All she'd wanted to do was curl up into a tight ball of misery and sleep for about six months, in the hope that when she woke up again, the pain would have gone away and the rest of her life would miraculously make sense.

But you couldn't do that. Children didn't let you.

She loved Abby and Tyler so much, and since leaving MJ she'd been feeling it in her heart and her stomach and her bones to an almost feverish extent. She wanted to hug them against her body fifty times a day. She wanted to gaze and gaze at them. Her marriage to MJ had been worthwhile a hundred times over, no matter how ugly their divorce might be, because of these two.

She'd been saying "I love you" so often that at one point yesterday Abby had sighed theatrically, put her hands on her hips and told her, "We know that, Mommy."

She loved them, but they were exhausting, and the little guilt monitor in the back of her brain kept telling her that she'd taken the easy way out, until now.

Taken the *trophy wife* way out, by leaving the kids with Maura or, before her, Kate and Robyn and Sveta, for hours and hours at a stretch, paying for endless mommy-and-me classes and toddler gym classes and toddler swim classes, so that—whether it was mommy and me, which it was sometimes, or Nanny and me, which it was too often— the kids were packaged into organized activities that left most of the real work to someone else.

Since leaving MJ was so much about not wanting to be a trophy wife anymore, she couldn't take the easy way out now.

Oh, she wasn't such an idealistic fool as to be attempting this without MJ's money behind her. She'd married him in the first place as an escape from the grinding poverty trap, and she had no intention of taking a step backward into the trap's evil jaws. But she was going to be as honorable about it as she could, taking only enough from him to ensure that his children were raised in the comfort and security he would want for them. Would insist on, in fact.

She wasn't awarding herself very many points for this attitude, right now, but, still, it was something. It was better than she'd seen from some of the other women in her circle—like Anna, for example, who'd openly spoken of taking her ex to the cleaners, whether to anyone else's eye the man deserved it or not.

The day went by.

Slow.

Boring.

Exhausting.

Punctuated by tiny diamond moments of *rightness* that she tried to lock into her memory to treasure later on. Abby singing a cheesy pop song to Tyler in the backseat of the car on the way to the store, her little four-year-old vocal cords valiantly attempting to mimic the electronic yodeling sound. Both of them with dabs of cookie dough on their noses when she let them lick the spoon and the bowl. The short-lived interlude of peace when they sat down at the table and ate the cookies, with milk for the children and a mug of steaming coffee for herself.

When Tyler went down for a nap, her first thought was simply "Thank heaven!" but when she turned to look back at him in the twin single bed that seemed so big for him and found his eyes already drifting shut, she had to pause and just watch him for a few moments because he was so precious and beautiful. His taffy-brown hair was so silky and fine on the pillow. His cheeks were so plump and pink.

They were so easy to love when they were asleep. Tyler would be giving up the daytime nap soon, because it had begun to push his bedtime at night later and later. For now, the time was precious. He was adorable…and thank goodness she had a break from him.

At six in the evening, just as she'd managed to get a home-cooked meal of spaghetti with meat sauce onto the table, there was a text from MJ. Coming tonight. Away early. Get to you nine-ish.

Tonight?

"There are *bits* in this," Abby said. She was frowning and indignant about it, and her blond ponytail needed refastening or she would end up with dinner in her hair.

"Sorry, sweetheart," Alicia said as she jumped up to rewind the bright pink elastic.

"Bits," Abby repeated, as she submitted to the procedure. "Of stuff. In the sauce."

So much for Alicia's attempt to insert stealth vegetables by chopping them up small. The weird thing was, Abby and Tyler both liked raw vegetable sticks with store-bought dips.

"It's just carrot and celery," she said, sitting down again.

"I don't like sara-lee."

"Yes, you do."

"Not cooked."

"Well, how about I put a blindfold on you, and then you won't know it's there." She jumped up again—even though her legs didn't want to move for a second time, with MJ's text still echoing through her mind and draining her strength—and pretended to get a dish towel to tie over Abby's face.

Abby giggled, and so did Tyler, and miraculously they forgot about those tiny-yet-sinister cubes of carrot and celery and ate their meal.

Which was a relief, because Alicia thought she would probably have put her head on the table and sobbed if they hadn't. It was a last-straw thing.

Because MJ was coming up tonight.

It seemed desperately important to get the kids into bed early, so that she would have a window of time—at least an hour—to compose herself, or firm her resolve, or rehearse what she wanted to say.

Change her clothes?

She looked down at her casual jeans, black ballet flats, white camisole and canary-yellow cotton cardigan. They didn't offer much in the way of armor or emotional protection. They didn't make a powerful statement. They said she was a mom at the end of a busy day. There was a smear of dried cookie dough on one sleeve of the cardigan, and the second button of the camisole seemed to be missing.

She should definitely change.

If there was time.

Because somehow, children seemed to have a sixth sense about when you were hurrying them off to sleep and they responded with the exact opposite behavior. At a quarter of nine, Abby was still calling out that her legs wouldn't stay still and she needed another glass of water.

Alicia delivered the water and then crept away, crossing her fingers that Tyler's peaceful breathing just a few feet from his big sister would soon lull her into sleep, also. She thought again about changing her outfit but then decided not to. The best armor was the reality of the situation, and reality tonight meant a stained top, a missing button and jeans.

Nothing to do, then, but listen and wait.

She paced the front room downstairs, unable to concentrate on anything except the increasing length of the silence from the children's room and the sound of the occasional car coming down the street.

But then when MJ arrived at ten after nine, she didn't hear him until his footsteps thudded onto the front porch. It was only the vehicles going past the house that made enough noise to be heard from inside the house, because they were traveling at a higher speed. When a car was slowing to turn in, it was too quiet.

She felt ambushed by his arrival, even though this wasn't fair.

Walking to the door, she was jittery all over, tense and short of breath and full of dread. He stood there just as he had the other night, back a little way, not stepping onto the coir doormat. He was dressed the same way he had been the other night, too, with his tie and suit jacket off and his shirt unfastened at the throat and rolled at the sleeves.

And he had her pillow in his arms.

He said awkwardly, "I thought you probably meant to bring this." He came forward and held it out and she took it and hugged it against her body, lost for words.

Her pillow.

The one she'd had ever since she could remember. The one she'd hand-sewn into a new cover, right on top of the old one, at least four times, because the old cover was falling apart. She always put two pillowcases on it now, to stave off its inevitable demise a little longer. This pillow had been her only companion in all of the moves she'd made. It had survived Grammie's death, and the foster homes, and the stars-in-her-eyes move to New York.

It had come into their marriage bed two days after they came back from Las Vegas, and she'd never told MJ why it was so precious, yet he'd never teased her about it or objected when she wanted to squash it into an already overfull suitcase when they went away.

Abby had been supposed to bring it down to the car, two days ago, but she'd forgotten the little errand, and Alicia had been so focused on writing the note to MJ, on wondering if it was the fair thing, and the best thing, or if they should talk, or if she should do it the twenty-first-century way and text. She only realized that she'd left it behind when she went to make up their beds here, that afternoon.

"Thank you," she said to him, with more emotion than was wise. She didn't want to be this moved that he'd thought of it, that he'd noticed and cared enough about such a small thing. And she didn't want him to see her emotion, but he did, and she knew it had given him a charge of satisfaction, as if he was adding up the points he'd scored.

"I'll grab my bags from the car," he said, with new energy. "I brought gifts for the kids."

"You shouldn't have."

"It was fine. I sent Carla out for them," he said over his shoulder, starting down the front steps.

"No, I mean you shouldn't do that, MJ, get into a pattern of giving them things to compensate for—"

"They're my kids. I have the right to communicate that I'm thinking of them."

"By having your office manager buy them each a gift?"

"Look, if you set a condition on any gift-giving that I have to do the shopping myself, then I will." He was still moving toward the car.

"I'm not setting conditions." She began to follow him, the pillow hugged tight in her arms. "We're getting distracted. This isn't what we need to talk about."

"We need to talk about a thousand things. A million things, Alicia." He rounded on her and came back up the steps, his anger rising. Beyond the anger, he looked tired and strained, with a papery quality to his skin and his dark eyes clouded. "I don't all that much care what order they come in. I'm getting my bags. Can you pour me a glass of wine?"

"Have you eaten?"

"Not really."

She knew what that meant—a stale roll or a muffin from one of the cafés at the hospital, eaten on the move. "You want me to fix you something? There's leftover pasta and sauce. I could throw a salad together."

"That would be great. Will you eat, too?"

"I'm not hungry. I ate with the children."

"Right."

So he brought in his bags while she took her precious pillow upstairs, reheated the mix of spaghetti and sauce and added the thick dusting of grated Parmesan that he liked. An outsider would never have guessed that divorce was in the wind, with such a typical division of day-to-day tasks.

But when she poured him a glass of wine, he told her, "Please have some, too. Join me in that, at least. How can we talk if I'm eating and drinking and you're just sitting there watching me? Or waiting on me?"

She poured another half a glass and they sat at the kitchen table.

"Did you tell the kids I was coming up?"

"I told them you were coming tomorrow. When I got your text, I…didn't correct that."

"Why not?"

"I thought I might not get them to bed."

"I would have liked to see them tonight. What time did they go to bed?"

"Tyler just after eight. He had a long nap. It's pushing back his bedtime. I wish I could still get him to bed at seven. Abby…" She didn't want to confess that there was a chance their daughter might still be awake. If MJ went up, and Abby heard him and wanted to come down—

They needed time to talk. It was good that he'd managed to get away tonight, even though at first she hadn't thought so.

Good in theory.

"Abby took a while to settle. But I haven't heard anything from her for the past hour." Slight exaggeration. Scrupulous honesty was overrated even in the best marriage, wasn't it? And theirs wasn't that.

"Why have you done this, Alicia?" he blurted out, low and intense. "Just tell me *why*. We can do something about it. Make changes."

"You want it in bullet points?" Because he made it sound way too easy, and she knew it was anything but.

"That is—" he laughed and shook his head "—not fair."

"Asking *why* isn't fair, either. I can't just—"

He looked down at the tangled coil of spaghetti and sauce on his plate, and then looked up again with an expression that was suddenly anguished, and came out with the last thing she would have expected, in a voice that didn't sound remotely like his own. "Okay, then I'll say it, Alicia, if you won't. Is it because there's someone else?"

"No! *No*, MJ!" The anger rose in her unexpectedly, and she swore—dark, nasty words she'd learned at her mother's knee and that Grammie had very thoroughly cut out from her vocabulary when she went to live with her at the age of five.

His face went still, as if she'd slapped him. "It's a reasonable question, isn't it?"

"It's a cliché!" But she was already regretting her reaction.

His whole body went still this time, and then he gripped the edge of the table. "No, it's not. It's an evil fear eating away at my gut, but if you want to dismiss it that way, as a mere cliché, go ahead." His eyes gleamed as if they were wet, and her heart thudded.

"There's no one else," she said. "I have all the time in

the world to find someone, but I'm not looking, so there's no one."

"You're saying it would be my fault if there was someone?"

"I think so. Yes."

"Even though you share so little of yourself with me that I—"

"*I* share so little of myself?"

Knots of tension appeared at his jaw. "All right, it goes both ways. I do know that. Neither of us shares enough. How do we change it?"

"We don't. At this point. If we haven't managed it by now…" Her throat hurt so much. "Seven years. That's a while."

"My parents have been married for thirty-eight years. They're still trying, still negotiating the partnership, as far as I can see."

"You're suggesting we should take your parents' marriage as a model?"

"It's a good one. At heart."

"The heart is buried deep."

"Do you trust something like a marriage when it's all on the surface? I don't."

He pushed his half-empty plate and his barely touched wine to one side and leaned forward, taking her hand before she could snatch it away. She'd been fiddling with her wineglass, running her fingers up and down the stem. It was a habit he'd noticed, apparently. Now he took advantage of the fact that her hand was right there for him.

"Pretense is easier than reality," he said, with a kind of urgency. "Reality does go deep. It does have layers."

He squeezed the hand he'd trapped in his grasp, and she let him, because she didn't want the distraction of snatching the hand away. When he realized she wasn't fighting him about it, he softened his grip and ran his thumb over her knuckles, back and forth in a gentle rhythm. Was he conscious of it?

"Isn't that a huge part of what you're saying about us?" he said. "That the deeper layers aren't there?"

He was making it so much harder than she'd expected. He kept reacting so much from left field.

Bringing her pillow with him.

Asking with such vulnerability about the possibility of another man.

Talking like this, instead of brushing her off as if he had far more important things on his mind, the way he so often did.

She couldn't stay at the table with him.

She didn't know the answer to his question. *Was* she saying that the deeper layers weren't there? She snatched back her hand, pulled away and stood up, making the chair legs scrape harshly against the tiled floor as she pushed it out from the table. "Are you asking me if I love you, MJ?"

"Oh, love!" he said, as if he questioned that the word had any meaning.

"Yes. Love."

"Do you? Love me?"

Don't ask me that now. It's too late. I'm the fool who brought it up.

"If I did, MJ, would I be asking for a divorce?"

"You might be," he said in a wooden way. "If this is all my fault."

"It's not," she answered quickly, because she knew it wasn't. "I'm not saying it's all your fault." She was the one who'd married him for his money, after all.

She stepped away from the table and turned her back to him, needing some time. He was throwing her off course, and if he sensed that, he'd try to take advantage. She knew it. He was a deal closer, a strategist, a winner. The only reason she was still in the room with him right now was because that side of him had been surprisingly absent from their interaction so far.

Behind her, he said quietly, "So if it goes both ways, if we're both at fault, doesn't that give us a chance? That's all I want, Alicia. A chance. For both of us. Maybe you've been thinking about this for a while, but I haven't. It never crossed my mind. I thought we were happy, where it counted. If we'd talked sooner, before you made up your mind... What's that stupid proverb? A stitch in time saves nine?" He laughed, as if he couldn't believe he was quoting proverbs to her, then said in a different tone, "I just want a chance."

She swallowed, and her throat hurt.

Decision time.

She could tell him to leave, insist that her decision was final and there was nothing to say. She'd been so certain that she was ready for it. But she hadn't expected him to fight for her this way.

Oh, that first visit on Wednesday night, yes, she'd absolutely expected that. She'd expected the anger and indignation and the sense of outrage that she was messing with his well-ordered life, ruining the outward appearance of perfection.

What she hadn't expected was the vulnerability and the willingness to listen.

What she'd expected even less was that these things would soften her so much.

She had almost said to him straight out that she didn't love him. Almost. *"If I did, would I be asking for a divorce?"* He'd almost said he didn't believe that love existed. Almost. *"Oh, love!"*

Maybe the existence of *almost* actually meant something.

Maybe there was some kind of love in there, somewhere.

She heard him get up from the table, then felt his hand come to rest on her shoulder. "Alicia…" He was appealing to her, not claiming her.

She couldn't answer. She was thinking back.

Chapter Seven

Seven years earlier...

Right up until the ceremony was over, Alicia was convinced they wouldn't go through with it. The effect of the wine would wear off, and MJ would realize that it was crazy to be doing this and that she'd somehow trapped him into it.

In the wedding chapel, she barely noticed a single detail of the atmosphere or the decor. She had to fight to hide the fact that her hands were shaking. He noticed how clammy they were and bent his head to her shoulder and whispered, "Are you nervous?"

"A—a little." More than nervous. Petrified that this would be her only chance and something would happen to snatch it away.

"You funny thing!" He laughed, confident and visibly sizzling with pride. "I'm not nervous at all."

That's the wine.

They'd only known each other for four months. Less. He knew she had nothing to offer but her looks. He didn't fully know the extent of her debts and her desperation because she hadn't told him, but she'd said enough to give him an idea. He knew she had no family. She wouldn't let him anywhere near her mean little apartment. He knew what she did for a living and that she'd given up her dreams of modeling or stardom.

He couldn't possibly really want this. Not with his full heart. Not for the right reasons.

"Are we ready?" the minister asked. He came as part of the package offered by the chapel, and as there was already another couple waiting for their turn, he wanted to move things along pretty fast. Alicia was only too happy to oblige.

"More than," she said.

"Can't wait," MJ agreed.

He was infatuated with her. That was a particularly ugly word, she'd always thought, but in this case it fit. She'd played him like a fish on a line, giving just enough to keep him interested and then pulling back. She'd held off nearly three whole months on sleeping with him, and that had tested her ingenuity and her people skills to breaking point.

If she had pushed it too far, he would have thought she was a frigid tease and would have lost interest. If she'd given in too soon, he would have thought she was too easy a prize and would have lost interest even faster.

She'd tied herself in knots this past winter, trying to play this whole thing exactly right. A beautiful woman needed to be a kind of mirror for a successful man. She needed to reflect back the image of himself that he wanted to see. He needed to feel so good about himself and his life when he was with her that he couldn't imagine anything better.

The minister was already reeling out the shortened vows. "I, Michael James McKinley, take you, Alicia Dream Smith..."

"Dream?" MJ whispered.

"I'm sorry. My mother was—"

"No, it's sweet."

She couldn't believe it was actually happening. She'd been holding her breath, incredibly superstitious, incredibly scared. When he'd given her the diamond hair clip tonight—oh, she had it in her hair right now, and it was so beautiful!—she'd thought that was it.

The end.

The goodbye gift to a temporary mistress.

She'd wondered what it was worth, and whether it would be enough to pay off her debts and finance her move from the city, maybe even pay for a part-time community-college office-management degree if she really stretched and scrimped for a few more years.

Then he'd said, "Let's get married," and she'd nearly cried with relief.

And now here they were. They repeated the last phrases of their vows, they put the plain gold bands on each other's fingers, and the minister told them they were husband and wife and invited the traditional kiss.

Alicia loved all the ways MJ kissed. Sometimes he was firm and hungry, sometimes gentle and slow, sometimes teasing. His whole mood and half his personality came through in his kiss, and she'd never known anything quite like that before.

She loved his kiss in this moment with her whole being, because they were *married* now, so she didn't have to second-guess every movement his mouth made on hers.

The meaning of his kiss wasn't make-or-break for her anymore. She'd made it already. She'd succeeded.

Tonight, his lips were smooth and soft and searching. It was the sweetest of kisses, a kiss with a promise in it, a slightly wine-tasting kiss. Only as they pulled apart did she wonder once more if the kiss would be happening without the wine.

Oh, did it matter?

They were *married*.

Back at the hotel, he ordered champagne and they had a hazy, silly and incredibly sexy wedding night that didn't get as far as sleep until four in the morning. MJ still seemed giddy and proud of what he'd done. He kissed her and touched her with a kind of triumph, and every movement he made, every taste to his skin, every sound, was perfect. She finally fell asleep in his arms as safe as a baby…safe…*safe*…and she felt so loved and so cherished, even though neither of them had said the words.

They'd said other things. *You are amazing. I love being with you so much. When I think about you, all I can do is smile.*

But they'd never said, "I love you."

Over a very late brunch the next day, MJ still didn't say it, but he talked plenty about what he planned. "I don't mind that you don't have a career, Alicia. In many ways, it's a plus. We're a partnership now, so there's no sense in doubling up. I can provide all the money and success either of us could want. You're the head of the support team." He laughed, looked at her, frowned with the smile still in place at the same time. "Sorry, I sound like the worst management consultant in the world. Do you mind that I see our marriage that way?"

"No, of course not."

What else could she say? What else could she *feel*?

After all, at heart she saw their marriage as a mutually beneficial partnership just as he did. His money and status would protect her from the vicious dogs of poverty and poor prospects snapping at her heels.

In return she would…well, she would do anything he wanted.

Chapter Eight

"Alicia. Please…" MJ said again. It was half a plea, half a command.

She didn't move. Neither his begging nor his ordering seemed to get through. He didn't know which attitude in himself he found most objectionable, the bossiness or the vulnerability. Both of them shocked him.

And he didn't know what she was thinking or feeling, how close she might be to wrenching herself out of his grasp. His hand felt like a lump of wood on her shoulder, inadequate and wrong. He wanted to do so much more. He wanted to hold her and kiss her and prove to her that they had something worth saving.

Was she open to that? Was it the right strategy?

Damn strategy! Damn the whole idea!

Before he could question anything more, he just did it. He took his heavy, dead hand from her shoulder and put his arms warmly around her. She was wearing straight-legged jeans that showed off the length of her legs and a bright yellow knit jacket-type thing that he'd seen before and loved for its sunny mood and the way it set off the gleaming blond of her hair.

Standing behind her, he felt her gym-toned body beneath the clothing, so graceful and willowy and perfect. His forearms nudged the undersides of her gorgeously rounded breasts in their covering of cotton and lace, while her flat stomach was soft yet elastic as he tightened his grip.

He couldn't let her go, and so far she wasn't fighting. She made a little sound in her throat and said his name. "MJ…"

The same way he'd said hers.

Helplessly. Emotions all mixed and wrong.

He put his chin on her shoulder and pressed his cheek against hers. The silky blond of her hair caressed his face and he smelled the delicious fragrance of her, a mix of shampoo and perfume. He loved the fact that she was beautiful, loved the care she took with her body and the delight she gave to every one of his senses.

If she'd been two inches taller, he had no doubt she would have made it as a model. She might have been the head of her own business empire by now, putting out a line of lingerie like Elle Macpherson or creating a successful television identity like Heidi Klum. She had a good head on those perfect shoulders.

But she'd never hinted that she wanted anything like that, and he was selfishly happy about her lack of worldly ambition. This way, all her energy and capability went toward her family and her community—himself, Abby and Tyler, his parents, her friends and the organizations for which she volunteered. He didn't know if his thinking belonged to the Dark Ages, or if it was a kind of feminism on his part, but he hated the fact that so many people dismissed the role of a woman at home.

What Alicia did every day *counted* for something, and the fact that she did it with plenty of paid help didn't detract from that. They could afford it. Should he force a heavy and unnecessary workload on her for no reason?

She had so many different roles and performed every one of them with care and commitment and good sense. She was no airhead, seriously, and she cared about education even though she didn't have much herself. Abby was almost reading already, because of the priority Alicia put on books and conversation and quality play.

Charity committees fell over themselves to secure her input when planning an event, because of her eye for detail. Mom loved her ideas about holiday celebrations, just the little flourishes in the menu or the activities or the decor, and when the two of them disagreed, Alicia was a good enough daughter-in-law to politely give way.

He was proud of her.

And she wanted a divorce.

Did she? She hadn't fought her way out of his arms. Hadn't even tried.

He slid his cheek along hers, to see what would happen and just because he couldn't help it, and she turned her face.

Not away but toward.

She nuzzled him and he searched for her mouth. A strand of her hair had fallen across her face, and it became part of their kiss until he reached up and tucked it away behind her ear. That was better. Oh, so much better. Here was her mouth, so sweet and familiar. He slid his hands up to her breasts, pushed aside the front panels of the cardigan jacket and cupped her through the much thinner cotton of the camisole top with possessive heat.

Her breasts were bigger since the children, and they'd always been on the generous side even before that. He had an unabashed male pride in their natural fullness.

Mine, guys, and I know I'm damned lucky.

He always thought that his hunger for her body reflected back onto her and aroused her, too. She loved what she did to him, loved that he was still so eager after seven years.

"Tell me we don't still have this," he whispered. She leaned back against him and made another sound in her throat. Conflict? Need? Loss? He didn't know.

"We barely have it," she said.

"What do you mean?" He kept planting kisses. On her jaw, on her lashes, on the corner of her mouth.

"We would already be done by now, most of the time."

"Done?"

"You only touch me in bed, and it lasts three minutes." She turned into his arms so she could look at him as she made the accusation. So she could see the effect of her knife in his guts? Was that the reason she was facing him now, when she hadn't faced him for their kiss?

It really hurt. "Three minutes?" he echoed hoarsely.

"Five? Six?" she drawled. Her arms came around his neck, cool fingers lacing behind his head. At the edge of his awareness, he saw that one of the buttons on her top was missing, giving a glimpse of the shadowed valley between her breasts. "Will I be generous and say it's seven?"

She pulled back and looked at him but kept her hands in place. Her eyes were as blue as a Swedish lake, but right now they were narrowed so that the blue only glinted between her thick, satiny lashes. She unlaced the fingers and curved her palm against his jaw in an uncertain caress, as if she wasn't at all sure why she was attempting to soften this for him.

"It's more than seven. Sheesh!" He leaned forward and pressed his forehead against hers, almost winded by the bluntness of this whole exchange. She'd never said anything like this to him before.

"Is that really the direction you want to go in, MJ?" she said now. "A pitiful argument about the exact length of our inadequate lovemaking?"

He took a ragged breath. It really, really *hurt*.

It hurt because he knew she was right. They had a pattern now, and it wasn't a good one. He fell into bed exhausted, and he needed the release before he could sleep. She gave it to him, and he gave enough in return for her to—

Something struck him. *Did* he give enough in return?

He said quietly, "Do you fake it?"

Every muscle in her body went tight, and she weighed her options for a silent moment so thick with meaning that he didn't even need to wait for her answer, because he already knew what it would be. "Yes."

"Since when?"

"Since Abby was born. Once or twice before that, I guess." She sounded strained and close to tears. She wasn't enjoying this.

Which was a plus, when you thought about it.

"How often now?" he made himself ask, although it felt as if he was taking that knife of hers to his gut with his own hand. "How often, on average, the past two years since we had Tyler?"

"Probably only about half the time. Maybe a little more."

"Only half or a little more. Thanks for telling me." He couldn't keep the bitterness away. He felt attacked to the depths of his being.

She wrenched out of his arms but didn't move away.

They could each have touched the other by moving a bare few inches. "Should I have lied again, then?" There was more appeal than anger in the question.

"Lied *again?*"

"A fake orgasm is a kind of lie, isn't it?"

"So why have you decided to tell the truth now, since you've been lying for so long?"

Another meaningful pause. "Because if we have any kind of a chance, then I need to be more honest."

He seized on what he wanted to hear—he knew he was doing this, even as it happened. "So you *do* think we have a chance?" He pressed the backs of his hands together in front of his sternum, fingers pointing upward. People told him he did that when he was lecturing to students, as a gesture of emphasis.

"I think I need to be more honest, whether we have a chance or not." Almost absentmindedly, she grabbed his hands and moved them down between their two bodies, as if she didn't want their lecturing presence getting in the way. The movement brought them so close again that he could feel her body heat.

"Do we have a chance, Alicia? We've—" Hell, he could barely get the words out. "We've started something big, here. I think. I know. Something important. We're talking. Being honest. You said it. I need to know. If your thinking has changed at all since you left me that note on Wednesday."

She shut her eyes, thumb and forefinger still circled around his wrists, down near her thighs. "Don't."

"Don't what? I could say the exact same thing to you, too. Don't. Just don't. Don't keep me in the dark. Tell me."

"Don't push me for…I don't know…a weather forecast. The percentage chance of rain. Don't push me to pinpoint the numbers on it. That there's a five-percent or a ten-percent chance we might stay together. You always want to win too quickly, MJ."

All right, he'd cop to that one. He liked to win, and he liked to know early on whether winning was likely. When it wasn't likely, he cut his losses and moved on. He'd done this with a particular surgical fellowship eight years ago, and people had told him he was crazy. "You still have a good shot at that one, MJ." But he'd assessed the odds and they'd come up too long for comfort. Instead, he'd focused on something a little less prestigious but where he had a better chance because of the personalities involved. He'd gotten it, and it had formed the basis of the career he had now.

"You're right," he told her, without misery or bitterness this time. "I see why you don't want to give percentages. That would…get in the way, wouldn't it?"

"Get in the way?"

"Of what we're trying to do—find a way through."

He waited for her to contradict him, to say what she'd said less than two days ago—that there was no possibility of a way through—but she stayed silent, and from this he took a tiny, precious jewel of hope.

They had a chance. They still had a chance.

The hope went to his head like alcohol and he made a stupid bid for certainty out of the confusion, played the wrong card. "I need you." He took a breath and announced—oh, yes, he could hear for himself that it was an announcement—"I love you, Alicia." He knew even before he'd said her name that the words were a huge mistake.

What was that? Alicia wondered cynically. His trump card? His winning play?

In seven years, he'd never said it, and now suddenly out

it came, despite that cynical "Oh, love" that he'd uttered earlier, and it made Alicia angry.

With him, partly.

With herself, more.

What a sucker you are, Alicia Dream Smith McKinley. What a sentimental sap. You want to believe him, don't you? You want to think it makes a difference.

The timing was way too convenient, and even though he'd said he wasn't trying to win right now, what else was saying "I love you" in this situation but a winning play?

Or an attempt at one, anyhow.

She wasn't falling for it.

"Love is not enough," she said.

He answered very seriously, "I know that," and she felt bad about her bluntness, as if she really might have hurt him with it.

"Love has so many meanings."

"I know that, too."

"You didn't even seem to want to admit its existence, a moment ago."

"I remember, believe me. And I asked if you loved me."

"Do you want an answer on that now?"

"Yes. I do. An honest one. Did you love me when you married me?"

If he wanted honesty… "I didn't give myself a chance to think about it."

He gritted his teeth. "Did you love me the day Abby was born?"

"With my whole heart."

"And Tyler?"

"The same."

"Do you love me now?" He bent his head, as if waiting for a blessing or a blow.

What answer could she possibly give? "I don't know.

And if that's…terrible, then I don't think what you're doing is any better."

"No?"

"You can say, 'I love you,' all you like to try to win this, but I'm not buying it, MJ. I'm sorry. I don't think either of us knows what we feel or what love even means in this situation."

"No. Maybe not. You're right. I said it out of—" He broke off and swore. "I was wrong."

"Well, we've both been wrong about a lot of things," she answered and didn't know if the words came from seven years of dutiful marital habit, her wifely role always to make him feel good about himself, or if it was a genuine concession.

Incredibly, they were still touching. Hands joined, bodies brushing lightly together.

Marriage did that, apparently. It made you so familiar with each other's bodies that you could hold each other and talk about divorce and the nonexistence of love at the same time. They stayed silent, nothing left to say on such a fraught subject. His hand whispered across her breast. His thighs pressed against her. His head was still bent, his chin not resting arrogantly on her hair, the way it so often was.

"Let me prove it doesn't have to take seven minutes," he said softly.

"No…"

"Why not?" Before she could say anything, he added quickly, "No, don't answer. I know what you'll say. That if we make love, I'll think it's more proof that I've won. I won't. I'm not that arrogant, Alicia. Not after what we've been through the past couple of days. And I'm not that shallow or that unthinking. I don't want to prove anything."

"Then what do you want?"

A thick beat of silence, while he struggled to strip back the layers. "I just want you. *You.* Your body against mine."

So simple. So tempting. And so honest that she couldn't doubt it.

He spread his hands over Alicia's backside through her jeans, buried his face in her neck, and heat bloomed powerfully in her lower belly. This was how it used to be, all slow and hot and delicious. Different every time. Unexpected in where it started or when it started or how it started.

Right now, they were just standing fully clothed in a kitchen in an old Victorian in Radford, Vermont, and the children were asleep, and the noises outside were so different from city noises, and for once she knew MJ wasn't thinking about a patient or a conference paper or a professional personality clash.

He was thinking about her and about making love to her, pouring his whole soul into it, after what they'd been through tonight, in a way that made her greedy and happy and weak.

Oh, she wanted it!

She shouldn't, it was crazy…just dumb…but she did. So much.

She closed her eyes, and the fight she should be making and the word she should be saying—*no!*—didn't happen.

Yes didn't happen, either, but he took her silence as agreement, and he wasn't wrong. He planted soft kisses on her earlobe and her neck, kept his hands in their cradling shape over her butt and traced the rounded shape of it that she knew he loved.

Close against his body, she could feel his arousal and it made her ache. She turned her face upward, wanting his mouth on hers, and he sensed her need at once and crushed his lips onto hers. She loved it when he kissed her this hard and this fierce. She loved that she could only kiss him back between hungry pants for breath and that she had to hold his face between her hands to keep him where she wanted him.

She kept expecting him to break off and drag her up to bed, but he didn't. He kept it open-ended and in the moment, and she loved that, too. She was tired of beds. Of the tidiness of them and the marital primness. Married people made love in bed. But her tired body so often insisted that beds weren't for making love at all; they were only for sleep.

He reached out and shut the kitchen wall lamp, and she whispered, "In the dark?"

"It's softer."

Softer, and more intimate. She felt closer to him in the darkness. The sense of safety and relief and escape from fear that he'd given her at the beginning of their marriage rushed over her again and she clung to him with shameless need, the fine cotton weave of his shirt smooth and faintly warm against her hands, from the heat of his body.

Don't stop. Don't stop.

He sensed that she'd given in completely, and peeled the cardigan jacket from her shoulders. She let it slip to the floor, let his fingers whisper against her collarbone as he unfastened the top button of her camisole. The second button was already gone, and it didn't take him long to tackle the rest. The camisole fell open all down the front and he lifted her breasts in their white lace bra and kissed the place where fabric met skin.

Her breathing frayed at the edges and she arched to meet the press of his mouth, nipples pebbled hard. He pushed her bra straps down and she helped him, unsnapping the hooks at the back in one impatient movement, so that seconds later she was standing there topless in the dark.

He pushed her back against the edge of the counter-top and spent forever on her breasts, his mouth hot on each nipple, his fingers tracing the fullness and lifting the weight, until she was sagging and lolling and melting, barely able to stand.

They didn't say a word.

Almost whimpering, she reached for him and fumbled with the front of his shirt until he was bare-chested like she was. She wrapped her arms around him and pressed herself into him, loving the way her nipples grazed the hard, sculpted expanse of his torso.

Gym visits deprived her of three extra hours of his company every week, but right now she didn't begrudge those hours because he had a terrific body beneath his serious professional clothing, and when they actually gave each other time—

The faked orgasms are my fault as much as his.

The realization shot into her like a dart and almost made her gasp.

"What's wrong?" MJ asked.

"Nothing is wrong."

"You flinched, or—"

"I—I want this," she said, heart full of remorse. "So much. So much. It can take all night."

He breathed something against her mouth that she didn't catch. Maybe just her name. It didn't matter. His body spoke louder, and the strength of the connection between them robbed her of any power to think. "I want you naked," she said.

"That's easy. You, too."

They scuffled and kicked and got rid of jeans and trousers and underwear and shoes, and she shivered for a moment until he held her again, which gave her all the heat she needed. Shedding their final pieces of clothing had broken the mood a little. They stood there in the stillness, bodies twisted together, their quickened breathing slowing down, the silence and dark of the night wrapping around them.

It could stop now. This was the moment where she could say no.

But still she didn't want to, and neither did he.

He kissed the top of her head and squeezed her hard, and she rested her ear against his chest and listened to his heartbeat. Then he began to touch her again, like playing an instrument. He knew the places. He knew the rhythm and the speed. He knew how to vary it, too, make it just that bit surprising and different. All the sketchiness and habit between them went out the window, and it was like new again.

He ran his finger lightly between her folds and she pushed into him, wanting more. He laughed and then groaned, grabbed her backside and let her know how ready he was. She made him wait—made *both* of them wait— by teasing him with the rock of her hips and the press of her breasts.

Finally, he'd had enough. He lifted her onto the countertop and she wrapped her legs around him and they came together. He filled her and she sheathed him and they fit together so perfectly, it was so different to those rushed, uncomfortable motions in bed when all MJ really wanted from her body was a way to get quickly to sleep.

So different.

She clung to him, arched and rocked against him, squeezed him, threw her head back and felt his hands on her breasts again. Oh, it was good. Oh, it was beyond thought or words.

When they came back to earth, he held her for a long time, while his breathing came back to normal, and then he lifted her down and held her again, more stiffly now, and she knew he wanted to speak. He took in a breath, then stopped. She could almost feel the words that were dammed back in his throat. He wanted to nail her surrender and make it into something that it wasn't—an end to this stupid talk of divorce, an admission that she'd been wrong about everything she wanted and everything she'd said.

She could imagine a typical line, the kind he flung at her when he was tired and couldn't be bothered mincing his words. *So does that put an end to this business?*

No, MJ.

Great sex doesn't solve what's wrong between us.

She waited, on edge, and he sensed the way she'd stiffened and loosened his hold on her. They turned out of each other's arms and she bent to find her scattered clothing, climbing into panties and buttoning her camisole but not bothering with the rest. She saw his gaze catch on the sight of her nipples through the thin cotton fabric and follow the bouncing sway of her breasts and the jut of her bottom as she bent again to pick up her jeans.

"So where am I sleeping?" he asked abruptly.

She froze, with her crumpled jeans and cardigan jacket bundled against her front, and then straightened slowly. "You want my answer to be the end of the whole thing, don't you? If I say the bed, with me—"

"Of course that's what I want, but if you don't want me to overinterpret, then I won't. If you don't want me in the bed at all, then I won't. I'll go in the study."

"Did you make a reservation at a motel, as I asked?"

Silence, then he said, "No, I didn't, in the end, after I realized I could get up here tonight."

"Because you were so sure this was just a whim."

He was angry now. "Have I for one second treated this as a whim? Maybe Wednesday night, yes, but since? Do me the courtesy of believing that I'm taking you seriously, Alicia. That I'm trying to work things out in the best way possible." He swore. "We've just pleasured each other on the kitchen countertop and now suddenly I'm the bad guy again? I didn't say a word!"

He was right. He hadn't. And she could hardly say that she'd heard the words from him anyhow, thick and unspoken in the air.

But he didn't actually *say* them, she reminded herself.

He was trying so hard. It wasn't fair of her to judge him on the basis of old patterns when he seemed to be fighting those patterns as hard as she was.

Harder, maybe.

And he was right, too, about the meaning of their lovemaking. It wasn't fair of her to do that, to respond so strongly to his touch and his taste and his smell, and then put him back in his place, as if he was a stranger in a bar harassing her with bad pickup lines.

"I'm sorry," she said and meant it. "I'll try not to react to things you haven't said."

"Thank you." He seemed to mean that, too.

"Sleep in the bed."

"Yes?"

"The kids will come in, in the morning. They'll be thrilled to find you there. They'll jump all over you."

Chapter Nine

The kids did come into the bed, they were thrilled, and they jumped. And squealed. And giggled.

They arrived at six-thirty, when it was light out but the sun hadn't yet risen and Alicia seriously wasn't ready to be awake. Abby would probably have slept a little longer, as she'd taken so long to settle last night, but her brother had woken her up and they showed up together, after the soft thud of their bare feet on the wooden floor had sent approximately twenty seconds of advance warning.

"Daddy!" Abby said. "Daddydaddydaddy!"

Tyler had to repeat everything his sister said anytime it struck him as fun, and saying, "Daddydaddydaddy" about a hundred times as if it was all one word, in his miniature Irish accent, was for some reason the funnest thing in the world. MJ scooped him up, rolled over and deposited him in the middle of the bed, and then Abby wanted the same treatment.

"Hiya, my two tigers." He laughed. "My two *Irish* tigers."

Alicia felt guilty and said in a quick aside to him, "They'll lose it now."

"It's cute, but, yes, they will."

"Why are you here?" Abby asked.

Separated from MJ by the children, Alicia saw him frown and shoot her a hostile look. *What did you tell them?* he mouthed.

She shook her head. Nothing. She'd told them nothing.

"What do you mean, sweetheart?" he asked their daughter.

"Why aren't you at the hospital? Why are you in the bed? In the mornings, Mommy is in the bed by herself and you're at the hospital. Don't you have any broken legs today?"

"Someone else is taking care of the broken legs, honey."

"Someone else?" Abby shrieked, astonished.

"Yes, another doctor."

"No! You're the only one who does the broken legs!"

"No, cuteness, there are lots of doctors who do broken legs, and arms, and other bones."

"Then how come they always leave all of them to you?"

"Well, they don't always. But I am pretty good at it, so when there are really difficult breaks, a lot of people want me to be the one to fix them."

"There better not be any difficult breaks today."

"No, you're right, there better not. Or tomorrow."

"You're staying *tomorrow?*"

"I'll go back in the afternoon."

"*Late* in the afternoon," Abby ordered. She was feeling her power. Her daddy was looking at her as if she was the most precious thing in the world, with one hand ruffling his son's hair at the same time.

Alicia's heart lurched. MJ loved his children. That was never in doubt. The ironic thing was, though, that if she went through with the separation, he would probably see more of them than he saw now. She and he would have to come up with a regular arrangement, a proper block of time, instead of him living in the same space as them but not seeing them awake for days at a stretch.

She'd seen this in other divorced couples she knew. The father went from odd snatched minutes of time with his children, usually with his wife on hand to bear the brunt, to the full sixty hours of every second weekend, on his own. She knew one divorced dad, in their wider circle, whom she was convinced had married again purely to provide himself with help on those long, difficult weekends.

If MJ did that—

Suddenly, a shaft of jealousy shot through her, shocking her to the bone. Could she really cope, seeing MJ with someone else? Someone who made him happy, when she and he had failed at happiness together?

It would be horrifically hard, she realized.

But that didn't mean she and MJ should stay married.

Abby was talking again—her habitual morning question. "What's happening today?"

"Let's ask your mom," MJ said.

All three of them looked at her, waiting for her verdict on the schedule.

She had no idea. MJ wanted to pack the weekend with family time, and quality time, and honesty time, as if relationships were a kind of concentrated orange juice, more efficiently managed in smaller containers.

Her mind did a couple of useful skips. From orange juice to apple juice. From apple juice to apple picking. It was fall, and Vermont was full of pick-your-own-apple orchards. "How about we go pick apples?" she suggested.

She met MJ's gaze, saw the appreciation and anticipation and relief. "That's a great idea."

Oh, it was! It chased that horrible vision of MJ in a second marriage from her mind.

"Apples! We're going picking apples!" Abby said. "We had that in a story at the library!"

Apparently it was a good story. Abby and Tyler were both yelling, "Applesapplesapples!" and bouncing on the bed. Alicia didn't remember the story, so Maura must have been the one to take them to library story time that day.

"Morning or afternoon?" MJ wanted to know, as if there was really any question. He honestly didn't know.

"Morning." You had to do it that way. Tire the two-year-old out in the morning, and he would nap better in the afternoon. Tire the four-year-old out, and she would be willing to play quietly while her brother slept.

"So we should get going."

"Well, no real hurry…" Because if you went on an outing *too* early in the morning, then you were home again too soon, with another few hours to fill in before the nap. You had to strategize this stuff with military precision.

She tried not to feel angry and resentful that, four years into fatherhood, MJ didn't know this. With Abby instructing Tyler to "Geroff t'e bed!" in her best County Cork lilt, she didn't have a leg to stand on in the resentment area. Alicia bit back the unjustifiable feeling and said instead, "I'm taking a shower, first."

The shower helped. She woke up and relaxed and thought about the day. It was sunny outside, crisp but beautiful, perfect apple-picking weather. If she could get a load of laundry into the machine before breakfast, it would be ready to hang out on Andy's outdoor clothesline before they left the house.

There was a dryer, also, but clothes dried in the open

air were a sensual treat, as far as Alicia was concerned. They belonged in the same, small precious group of things in her life where her pillow also fitted.

When she emerged from the shower, she heard MJ downstairs with the kids. "Want to shake it now, Tyler? Yes, that's right."

"No, Tyler, you have to shake it harder!" Abby said.

Shake what?

She dressed quickly—black pants, figure-hugging scoop-necked stretchy top with a flower pattern, cute dusty-pink jacket—because she was a little curious about what was happening down there. When she arrived, she found pancakes in progress, from the shake-up mix she'd bought the other day. MJ had found it in the pantry, possibly led there with evil intent by his daughter.

He stood at the stove and turned to grin at her when she walked into the kitchen. He had a pancake flipper in his hand and a plastic barbecue apron covering his clothes and he looked sexy and relaxed and in control…and infuriatingly—if also cutely—pleased with himself about the fact that he was cooking. Once more, she had to swallow a snarky reaction.

It's going to take more than one Saturday pancake breakfast, MJ.

But he knew that, she reminded herself. He did. *Be fair, Alicia.*

Fair was the hardest thing in the world.

"Flip them. They're ready," she told him, seeing the cluster of popped bubbles on top of each one.

"Want to take over?" He began to turn the pancakes, and they were already a little overcooked, edging to dark brownish-black instead of golden in a couple of places.

The mood teetered on the edge of hostility and criticism: *he* couldn't cook pancakes, while *she* was putting him down about it.

"Nope," she answered lightly, dragging it back from the brink. "I'll make the coffee, shall I?"

"Sounds great." He injected the same ease and warmth into his voice, and she knew they'd both passed a small but important test.

Kindness, that was such a big part of it. They needed to be kinder to each other, give each other the benefit of the doubt. Find the manners and the warmth, instead of jumping at once to the most negative option in their interactions.

She made coffee and squeezed some oranges for fresh juice, took Tyler to the bathroom, then threw a bundle of laundry into the machine, while MJ plated up the pancakes with a flourish—swirls of syrup, dustings of powdered sugar and a cluster of blueberries on the side.

They sat at the kitchen table and ate, with Tyler making a mess and Abby chatting happily, both kids still in their pajamas. The whole meal belonged on a Norman Rockwell platter, too good to be true, but that was okay. They didn't have to rush to the heart of things all at once.

They couldn't, with the children around.

MJ had cleared away the meal by the time Alicia finished supervising the kids with getting dressed and brushing teeth. "So we're ready to go?" he said, striding forward to meet her in the front room, while the kids scuffled together at the foot of the stairs.

"Not quite. I want to get the laundry out, and it hasn't started its final spin yet."

"Can't we leave it in the machine and then throw it in the dryer when we get home?"

"I want to hang it outside." She turned and headed in the direction of the laundry room to see how many min-

utes were left in the cycle, displayed on the electronic
control panel.

"Why, Alicia, when there's a perfectly good dryer?" he
asked impatiently, following her. "That's going to mean
waiting another, what, fifteen minutes for the cycle to
finish…"

"Seventeen," she corrected, seeing the panel.

"…and then another ten hanging it out. Nearly half an
hour." The machine was rinsing at the moment, chugging
energetically back and forth, with water sloshing. It probably wasn't a sound MJ heard all that often. He'd had to
raise his voice above it.

"It's not even nine o'clock," she answered him. "Are
we in that much of a hurry?"

"It'll take another half hour driving to the apple farm,"
said the man who worked a ninety-hour week and didn't
tolerate the slightest time-wasting or inefficiency as a result.

The old Alicia would have obediently stopped arguing
at that point. The new Alicia wasn't sure that she should.
On the other hand, there was the kindness thing. Where
did you find the right balance?

They faced each other, with the chugging washing machine looking on, and once more they teetered. Hostile
or kind?

She said carefully, "Can I please tell you why I really
like to hang laundry outside? I don't get to do it all that
often." Living in Manhattan? Please!

He answered, carefully also, "Please do tell me. Since
this seems to be turning into something important." He
leaned the heel of his hand on the vibrating machine, ready
to listen.

She took a breath, suddenly didn't want to say it but was
committed now. "Grammie used to do it. She never even

had a dryer. Which in winter and rainy weather sometimes meant we had clothes hanging all over the heating vents. But most of the time she hung it out, and by the time I was seven or eight I was helping her bring it in, and, oh, Michael, the smell and feel of it!"

"Really? That good?"

"Especially cotton sheets. When she got sick and was having the treatment and was so nauseous, there were so few things that she could stand to smell, but that was one of them that still gave her pleasure. I used to have to bring her the basket, with the fresh dry sheets bundled in there, and she'd put her face right to them and inhale. I still do that. Every time. It reminds me of her. Oh, shoot, when I say it, it sounds like such a little thing."

"No," he said, then repeated more urgently, "no, it doesn't sound little at all. It sounds— I can see now. Of course we'll wait and hang out the laundry." He swore. "We never talk like this, do we? I know your grandmother was important to you, but we've barely talked about your memories of her. Or my childhood. Or anything. We need to! We need to start."

"You can't just turn it on. You can't just…start talking." They were still facing each other, like heads of state across a negotiating table, totally focused, very wary, willing to listen.

"You can," MJ insisted.

"How?"

"Make a game of it."

"A game?" She laughed.

But he meant it. "Every day, we should pick a topic and we have to share three things about it."

"Three favorite childhood memories."

"Yes. Exactly."

"Three most terrifying moments."

"Those, too." He lowered his voice and brushed his fingers against her cheek. "Three things I love about the way you kiss."

He wanted to kiss her right now, but she couldn't let it happen. If she did, all they would think about was the kiss, and it was the other stuff in this interaction that was important.

No, kissing…sex…was important, too, but she thought they'd made more progress with that than with the rest. Last night had been— Oh, when she remembered, when her body remembered, she shivered and melted inside.

She looked at MJ's mouth and wanted it so badly. It was so close. He watched her watching him and again— *again!*—they teetered but for a different reason.

"Three things I love about the way you kiss, too," she said in a strained voice, but then the washing machine switched abruptly to its spin cycle, and the load was unbalanced, and the whole thing began to shake and thump before sorting itself out and getting faster and smoother the way it should.

Well, that was marriage for you. Three things about the way they kissed, and a washing machine for a chaperone.

A washing machine and two children. They heard the bump of a head on wood, and Tyler began to cry.

"Maybe we should get to the three things later," MJ said.

"Uh, yeah, I think so." She was breathless as she rushed to check that Tyler was all right.

He was. Just a minor bump on the head. MJ always said that if they cried with that much energy right away, there was no damage done, and that it was silence after a bump that should worry her. When the wash cycle finished, they hung out the laundry together.

Then they went apple picking.

It was the perfect day for it, as she'd thought first thing this morning. The shadows beneath the trees were cool and blue, the air fresh and fragrant. Two huge Clydesdale horses transported them, along with three other family groups, in an open wagon with hay bales for seats to the distant rows of apple trees. Abby and Tyler had never been in a horse-drawn vehicle before and they loved the slow, rolling movement and the sight of the big, shaggy beasts upfront. The ride was over all too fast, and Alicia thought that the photos MJ captured on his phone—they'd forgotten to bring the actual camera—would only convey a fraction of the flavor of her memories.

Let loose among the apple trees with their red plastic buckets, the kids went crazy. MJ had to explain to Tyler that the fruit already fallen on the ground might not be good to eat, and he almost cried when his half-filled bucket was upended, but MJ was right. Several of the apples had been on the ground too long and had begun to rot.

"Can't reach!" Tyler said about the apples still on the branches.

"You can now," MJ answered, swinging him up onto those strong shoulders and moving carefully between the branches so that neither he nor Tyler got scratched or bumped.

Abby didn't want any help. She stretched valiantly upward and could reach enough of the apples on the lower branches to satisfy. They ate as they picked, and were torn between the three varieties, golden delicious, northern spy and idareds. They were all delicious and so fresh, picked right off the tree.

"Are we really taking home four buckets of apples?" MJ wanted to know, as Abby's and Tyler's baskets filled higher and higher. "Can we eat that many?"

"I'll bake," Alicia said.

"Oh, you will?"

"Cooking is good, with the kids. It takes twice as long, true, but they love to help…and taste. We don't have so many organized activities up here as we had in the city. It can be a challenge to find things to do all day."

But he wasn't so interested in the challenge of filling the hours. Alicia wasn't sure that he'd heard what she'd said.

"That apple pie we had a couple of weeks ago," he was saying, "did you make that?"

"The one I left for you after you had that emergency come in at noon and didn't get out of surgery till two in the morning?"

"Yes, and I was starving and ate almost the whole thing."

"Yes, I made that."

"Wow."

"Did you not think I made it?"

"I didn't know. I thought Maura or Rosanna, or a bakery."

"A bakery?" She was surprised he couldn't tell it was home-made.

He shrugged and looked a little embarrassed. "Alicia, I never know where the food comes from."

"You could ask."

"I'm asking now. Do you cook much of it? Do you like to cook?"

"I cook some. I do like it. I also like picking up the phone and ordering in. I like being able to choose."

"How many meals that we eat—evening meals—would you have cooked in a week?" He was looking at her as if he'd never seen her before, and it made her blush. There was so much in his expression—heat and fascination and apology.

She answered him helplessly, not knowing quite what

he wanted or how much detail. "Probably only one or two. It varies. I like baking best. Desserts and cookies are mostly home-made. Casseroles and pasta sauces, not so much. Maura used to make stews. Rosanna makes Caribbean food. That pelau thing that you like, that's hers." She couldn't believe this weird conversation. "But you knew that, didn't you? You must know which things I've cooked and which I haven't, which things come from a restaurant or the deli, or someone else."

"No, I don't."

"Really?" They looked helplessly at each other. "H-how can that have happened?"

"You're saying it's my fault."

"No. No, I'm not. I think it has to be both of us. Not communicating. Making assumptions. Not being interested enough."

"Interested enough?"

"In each other's lives. The hours you work make us very separate, don't you think?"

"What choice do I have about the hours?"

She ignored that. "And I don't ask enough about your day, and you don't ask enough about mine."

"Okay, so let's start the game. Right now."

"Right now?" She looked around, but Abby was still happy hunting for apples. Tyler's bucket swung in MJ's hand, while Tyler himself was running on the grass between the orchard rows.

"Yes. Tell me your three favorite things to bake. We can have fun with this, can't we?" He smiled at her, the kind of smile that made his practice's medical secretaries work three hours late just because he asked. "Doesn't have to be just our three darkest fears."

Her awareness of him flared and made her flustered. How could she melt inside like this, when she was planning their divorce with the same hardheaded calculation she'd used to plan their marriage? What was wrong with her?

"I guess it doesn't. Okay, let's see…" she said, battling to keep on track. "Pumpkin pie, chocolate-chip cookies and crème brûlée."

"Huh. Okay."

"Now it's your turn."

"I don't bake."

"Yeah, really?" she drawled. "I mean your three favorite baked treats to eat."

"Crème brûlée, raspberry tart and any kind of layered Vienna-style torte with a kick of alcohol in it. But pumpkin pie and chocolate-chip cookies are pretty good, too."

"I think I have a German cake book somewhere. Those big tortes are hard, though, a real project, not a spur-of-the-moment thing."

"We had one match, the crème brûlée."

"If you knew how much cream was in that…"

"I think my cholesterol level can survive. Is it hard to make?"

"No, it's easy. Four ingredients. Eggs, cream, sugar, vanilla. Just needs a little patience so it doesn't curdle. And a blowtorch."

He laughed. "A blowtorch. You're kidding me."

"No, for real. A special kitchen one, to caramelize the sugar on top, to get that hard glaze."

"That's the best part, so brittle and sweet, with the soft…"

But Alicia stopped listening at that point.

Tyler had just disappeared around the end of a row of apples and she'd lost sight of him. She quickly turned and stepped around the opposite end of the row and found him running toward her. She held out her arms but he decided it was a game of chase and turned to run back the opposite way. She saw the horse-pulled wagon coming along the track with its next load of apple pickers and—you had to do this—anticipated the possibility that Tyler would run out between the rows and onto the track at the worst possible moment.

She broke into a run to catch up to him. "Tyler! Stop!"

He thought it was part of the game and only went faster, and she was breathless by the time she ran him down and scooped him up. It hadn't been a near-miss or anything like that. The two horses were still a good ten yards distant and Tyler would probably have seen them and stopped, or the wagon driver would have halted his animals, but you couldn't take the chance. Tyler was an accident waiting to happen, every single day.

"Hey," MJ said behind her, "weren't we in the middle of something? You just left." Alicia turned. He stood there, a little indignant, hands held defensively away from his body with the buckets of apples swinging. Then he saw the horses come into view behind her, between the apple trees, and registered the presence of Tyler in her arms, wriggling to get down. "Okay, right, sorry. You thought he was going to run under their hooves. I forget what it's like sometimes."

"With the brittle caramelized sugar and the soft, creamy part underneath. I know."

"Huh?"

"What you were saying. Before we were interrupted."

He laughed. "You put me on the pause setting."

"Yep."

"I'm going to have to learn to do that."

"I'm sorry, MJ. Multitasking conversations is a gift. I think you either have it or you don't."

He laughed again, and their gazes held, and the moment was…oh…nice. The whole conversation about baking had been pretty nice.

But then Abby came up to them with her bucket of apples so full the top three or four would tumble out at any moment. Alicia took them quickly and put them in her own bucket.

"Shall we take this ride back?" MJ asked. "Our buckets are full." The new arrivals had climbed out and the wagon was empty, the horses standing patiently until they had a load of passengers for the return journey.

"Let's not hurry. It's so beautiful here. We could walk down the hill a little to the other pickup point and get the next ride."

MJ nodded, and she could see him making the effort to slow down, as he realized there was no reason or benefit to rush, the way he usually did all day. The air was sweet with the smell of fresh apples, and Abby and Tyler had a ton of energy left to burn. There was a wooden bench at the far end of the rows. Alicia and MJ sat there together while Abby and Tyler turned the fallen fruit into toys, making precarious towers and snaking lines.

MJ said quietly to her, "We did an easy one, with the three baking things. Can we try a harder one now?"

"Okay."

"Three scariest childhood moments."

"Oh, great! You first, this time."

"That's fair." He thought for a moment, then told her about taking a boat trip on Lake Champlain and almost slipping off the ramp, down into the dark water between the dock and the boat's side, and about having a brown recluse spider crawl over his leg, during a vacation in Arizona. "And once when I came into a room and Mom was crying and I didn't know why, and she wouldn't tell me right away—my grandfather, Dad's father, had died, and

Dad didn't know yet and she thought he should know first. And I was old enough to imagine worse things than that."

"That's a different kind of fear, isn't it, from the first two?"

"Very. But all three are pretty vivid."

"Mine aren't," she said.

"No?"

"They're blurred. I can't talk about three, or four, or ten. They're all about Mom, and they're all mixed up together." She sketched it out—the times Mom left her alone in the apartment when she was three or four years old and didn't give a firm time about when she was coming back; the times Mom behaved strangely, or yelled, or pushed her away. "And then when I was with Grammie, I can't remember a single time when I was scared, until she got sick, and then I was scared all the time." She kept her tone deliberately light.

"You don't talk about these things."

"What is there to say? It was a long time ago. You can guess what it would have been like. I'm a poster child."

"Guessing isn't detail. Guessing doesn't let me see you in the poster, Alicia."

"I didn't think you'd want to know detail. And I don't want to go on dragging my past with me. It's gone now. It's done."

"It formed you, made you the person you are now. Makes me proud of you."

"Yeah?"

"Yes, Alicia."

She said lightly, "Well, that's something."

One of the orchard staff came along with a long-handled scoop and a cart to collect the windfall apples up.

Alicia held her breath. Were the children going to protest the end of their game?

But, no, apparently the sight of the scoops of apples going into the cart was interesting enough as a distraction. So many apples!

"What happens to those?" Abby asked the stranger. She was always curious about anything new. Smart as a tack, Alicia thought, which was no surprise, considering the brains in MJ's family.

"We make them into juice," the man said cheerfully.

"Mommy said we're not allowed to eat the fallen ones."

"Well, your mommy is right, if they have bad spots, but we pick out the bad ones and clean the good ones before they go into the machine."

"Can we see the machine?"

"No, I'm sorry, sweetness. We don't allow that."

"Oh. Okay."

"But we sell the juice."

"Mommy, can we buy some apple juice?"

"We'll stop in the gift shop and see what they have, shall we?"

They set off down the slope. Tyler fell once, attempting to keep up with his sister, but he wasn't hurt in the thick grass and soft soil, just a little smeared with green and brown. Alicia brushed him off as they waited at the stop for the horse-drawn wagon.

The ride back to the gift shop took a different route to the way they had come and lasted a little longer, and it was one of those times when you wouldn't have minded if the world had ended right there because it was so perfect, Alicia felt. MJ's shoulder bumped gently against hers with the movement of the wagon, the contact a physical echo of the fact that for now at least they were at peace with each other. The kids were happy and tired enough to sit contentedly in laps—Tyler in hers, Abby in her daddy's—and she began to think about what they might buy and what she might bake.

Apple upside-down cake, apple pandowdy, apple bread, apple muffins…

MJ bought her an old-fashioned frilly apron with a lush red-and-green apple print, and she bought him a porcelain apple-shaped pencil holder. Abby begged for one of the candy apples until she discovered they were really candy apple *soaps*—at which point, she begged for them harder. So they bought two of those, also, one for each of the children.

And they bought a gallon of juice.

"We're going to apple these kids out to the point where they'll never eat another one," MJ predicted.

"We can freeze some of the juice and some of the things I bake."

"Do any of the things you bake get to come back to the city?" he asked casually, but as soon as the words were out, it became a loaded question about the state of their marriage and they both wished he hadn't asked.

"Tell me what you'd most like to take with you tomorrow, and I'll bake that today," she said, careful and polite.

But he ignored the safe way out that she'd offered them both. "I'm coming up again, Alicia, whenever I can get the time," he said, quiet and low. They stood in the middle of the gift shop, purchases already paid for and arms full, while the children took a last look at the Halloween section of the store. "Until you tell me you don't want me, I'm going to keep coming."

She couldn't stop the bitter comment that escaped her lips. "It's taken my leaving you to make you start trying?"

"If you're saying I should have made this kind of time for my family long ago, pushed us to talk about important stuff long ago, then I accept the criticism, but do you know what? You never, ever made me feel that you wanted more of me. I thought—" He broke off suddenly, blinked and swallowed, and she was so shocked that she didn't know how to follow through.

MJ? This emotional? Again? They were in public. It was impossible.

That very second, Tyler suddenly went from innocently studying pumpkin night-lights to picking up a fragile-looking set of Halloween-themed shot glasses. She got to him just in time, and then he needed an urgent bathroom visit, and what MJ thought—the thing that had made him struggle to master himself—couldn't take priority.

Not here. Not now.

"Later," she said. But he didn't answer. He was taking Abby by the hand and she couldn't see his face.

Chapter Ten

"Dr. McKinley, I wouldn't normally have called you about something like this—" said Raj Mistry on the phone.

"No, I hope not, whatever it is, because I specifically asked to be kept free of calls this weekend," MJ interrupted.

He was on edge. Alicia was upstairs putting Tyler down for his nap. Abby had a cartoon DVD playing in the front room and was tired enough to be sitting still and quiet while she watched it. It was three in the afternoon, a good two and a half hours since MJ's interrupted conversation with Alicia in the apple-orchard gift shop, and as soon as Tyler had closed his eyes they would have to finish that talk.

He needed to say it. *You married me for my money.* He needed to find out how she would respond to the accusation. Maybe even more, he needed to feel his own reaction to whatever she said. Except that he knew already, didn't he? No matter how much he'd always believed it, hearing her say it would cut him to the core.

It hadn't hurt him to believe it at first. He'd felt like a knight in shining armor, coming to her rescue, and that was a romantic, heartwarming idea. He'd unconsciously seen his own brilliant knightly self turning her gratitude and relief into a deep and all-consuming love through his sheer all-around fabulousness within months of their wedding, and, yes, he was mocking himself.

Bitterly mocking himself, because he'd been so wrong. The transformation of relief to love had never happened. He wasn't that fabulous, after all.

"They called me down to the E.R. for a serious road trauma case," Raj was saying. "You won't believe who the patient is."

"Who?" he asked, obedient to Raj's cue because, to be honest, he wasn't really thinking about it. He was thinking about his marriage, pacing the kitchen, making a poor attempt at tidying away the mess from their late lunch with his one free hand.

"Hannah Majeska."

He came to a halt in the middle of the room. "No."

"I'm afraid so."

MJ could count on the fingers of one hand the patients for whom he felt this degree of personal care and responsibility, and Hannah Majeska was probably at the very top of the list.

Hannah was nine. She'd been born with serious abnormalities in the bones of her legs, and it had taken several significant procedures over several years to correct them. She was such a brave kid, so funny and bright and strong. Her parents were the best people in the world—loving and sensible, unfailingly cooperative with medical staff, endlessly patient with painful waiting, unexpected setbacks, a thousand different follow-up appointments.

And now she'd had a car crash.

"How is she?"

"Pretty broken up, but no head injuries and the abdominal bleeding is under control. They're removing her spleen."

"Fractures?"

Raj listed them—pelvis, ribs, both femurs—then added, "The parents are asking about you. They want you. They trust you. They're shattered, obviously. I didn't know what to tell them."

"Tell them I'll be there tonight," he said, without even thinking about it. "Tell them to call me before that, if they want to. Give them my cell-phone number."

"I'll do that. Good." Raj sounded relieved that MJ wasn't biting his head off. MJ ended the call quickly, shoved his phone into a pocket and saw Alicia coming through from the front room.

"You're leaving?" she asked. Her face had that well-schooled blankness to it that he realized he saw far too often, and she'd obviously heard the end of the phone conversation.

"It's a patient," he began awkwardly. "A really unique patient."

Hell, had he ever talked about Hannah to Alicia? Probably not. He hardly talked to her about his work at all, ever, even when it was extra important or difficult. *Especially* when it was. He valued the separation. Needed it, the way she needed to put her difficult past behind her. Even though he had probably never explained that to her, either, or made the connection. And today it was biting him in the butt. He floundered through an explanation that didn't begin to cover the full story.

"Anyone else and I wouldn't be doing this," he added. "There are other doctors, despite what Abby thinks. Alicia, you're angry, aren't you?"

"Not that you're going, if this little girl and her parents need you that much. How could I be that selfish?"

"Then what's the problem?"

She searched for the right words and his heart sank at how hard this was, how careful they had to be. They were in the middle of a minefield, and the smallest misstep of a wrong word choice could set off an explosion that might— easily—end everything.

"Couldn't you have run it by me first?" she asked. "Even if it was just a token? Even if you'd already made up your mind to go? You say we're a partnership. You've always said that. I—I don't mind the business comparison, I guess. Except that it doesn't feel like a partnership. It feels like the kind of partnership I had with Maura."

"With *Maura?*" He followed the implication pretty fast.

They had the same relationship as an employer and an employee, Alicia was saying. One of them made the decisions, the other nodded and went along. Until the breaking point came—as it had done just a couple of days ago for Maura—and when that happened, the employee felt no obligation and no regret. She could just waltz out of the employer's life without guilt or a backward glance.

"That level of inequality?" he blurted out.

Alicia closed her eyes and nodded, her mouth pressed tightly shut and her lashes as always long and dark and silky against her cheeks. He wanted to step across the space that separated them and just pull her into his arms and tell her it was crazy, it was nonsense, but that was such an *unequal* thing to do, dismissing her opinion and her feelings like that. It played right into the bedrock of her concerns.

This was what happened in unequal partnerships. One person talked, the other listened. One person said how things were, the other person pretended to agree, even when they were a seething mass of rebellion inside.

Alicia's obedience and dutifulness and accommodating attitude all these years suddenly stopped being a sign of the health and happiness of their marriage and became the symptom of the exact opposite.

He'd told Raj he was coming back to the city and would see David and Louise Majeska tonight, and it was already after three. Hell, if he and Alicia tried to pull this apart now, how long would it take? He didn't want to start something that might end worse than it began, if they didn't have the time and headspace to really follow through. He felt the minefield risk of it once again, like something physical, as if he was bound in barbed wire or strapped to a bomb.

"I'm sorry" was all he could say. He felt he'd said it a hundred times already and it wasn't getting them anywhere. "I'll remember that next time. I'll consult you. I'll talk to you."

"Please, yes."

"I can call Raj back, ask him to tell the Majeskas I can't be there until tomorrow."

"No, don't do that. Go. I understand."

"Do you?"

"Let's talk about that sometime. Whether I really do."

"That's a threat."

"I guess it is, in a way." She sounded so detached. The way Maura apparently had been when she'd announced that she was leaving.

His head began to ache and he felt a spurt of anger.

I don't have time for this.

He had to work so hard not to snap the words at her, to

consider her point of view. It was like turning a huge ship in midocean. *Count to ten, MJ. Count to twenty. Think about what's happening here. Think about what she's saying and why you're angry.*

He realized it was an attitude he projected a lot—this expectation that everything on the home front would run without a hitch or even an inconvenient mood on his wife's part. That was the bargain, wasn't it? He gave her the security and the free rein to spend, and in return she solved every problem, squashed down every protest, blanked out every emotion that didn't fit.

"I'll be back up as soon as I can," he said, and it was as much of a threat as her *"Let's talk about that"* line had been.

When he'd gone, and when Alicia had dealt with Abby's lengthy tears at his going, she sank onto the couch beside her daughter, swamped by a level of fatigue that suggested she'd run a marathon. She and MJ were both trying so hard, and she wasn't sure that she knew why.

Well, because of the children—this precocious little being beside her, attention once more glued to her Disney DVD, and the other one still sleeping upstairs.

But, no, if it was only because of the children, then it wouldn't work.

The children were important. The most important beings in the world. Whether she and MJ split up or stayed together, she would tie herself in knots to avoid modeling a bad relationship for them. She wanted them to believe in love—in the important things about love, like generosity and forgiveness and compromise.

But how much of a lie could you live, and how long could you live it for before you damaged yourself so much that the damage spilled onto your kids like acid and hurt them even worse than a divorce?

Do you want them to believe in magic?

The question echoed in her head as abruptly and unexpectedly as if someone was standing in the room asking it out loud. Or as if someone had identified the missing ingredient in her recipe for love and wanted her to fix the mistake before she put the thing in the oven to bake.

Magic.

Did you need magic?

Did it even exist?

Back in Las Vegas, or on the early vacations she and MJ had taken together before the kids, had there ever been any magic? *Not for me,* she realized bleakly.

She hadn't let herself feel that kind of nonsense. The world could be a cold, hard place, and just for once it had cut her a lucky break. She'd been so caught up in her relief and triumph at having the ring on her finger, and so determined to cement the deal by being the most perfect wife imaginable, she'd never relaxed enough to let magic anywhere near her.

She knew she needed to hold on to MJ for at least two years, she had calculated, or she wouldn't have much hope of coming away with enough of a divorce settlement to live on. She couldn't afford to have him tire of her or see through her too fast. She had to stay on top of her role and what he wanted from her. She had to perform like an Oscar-winning actress.

There was no room for magic in any of that.

And yet love's magic *was* real.

She believed that.

What else could explain the way Grammie's care had wrapped around her and healed her from the broken years of her mother's drug addiction? She barely remembered her mother, having lost her to an overdose when she was only five.

She'd lost Grammie, too, just five years later, and it had to be the magic of love, and her memories of it, that had kept her going during the bleak and messy seven years that followed. Out of the three foster homes she'd been in, just one, the Brownlows, had given her another glimpse of love, but she hadn't been able to stay permanently with that family. She'd known going in, at the age of fourteen, that it would only be a temporary thing.

Still, rediscovering that magic, seeing the love in the Brownlow family, even if only as an outsider, had given her another dose of hope.

This hope hadn't left her. This hope and magic was sitting right here on the couch with her, in the form of Abby snuggled against her.

"I love you, baby girl," she said.

Abby sighed. "Oh, Mommy! Are you saying that again?"

"Well, yes, I am."

"Why do you have to keep saying it?"

Because it helps.

"Because it just slips out."

"You're only allowed to say it at bedtime, okay?"

"Oh, I am?"

"When you tuck me in and kiss me."

"Okay, if that's what you want. I'll just say it at bedtime when I tuck you in."

See? There! The magic of love, woven into Abby's absolute and total confidence that she would be tucked in and kissed every night when she went to bed. Maybe Abby was right that Alicia didn't have to keep saying it. Maybe it didn't matter that she and MJ never said it to each other.

Maybe it was there, and everything it needed to be, with-out the words....

But on this one, she wasn't nearly so sure.

MJ texted twice over the next six hours and called her late at night, once he was finally back at the apartment. "Kids asleep?" He sounded almost asleep himself.

"Yes, since eight-thirty."

"So how have you spent the evening?" It was nearly ten-thirty now.

"Baking."

He laughed. "Aha. Of course. But I thought you were going to do that with the kids."

"We made apple pie in a state of chaos. Now I'm doing apple bread in peace."

"Slice it and toast it for breakfast?"

"Actually, that's a good idea."

"I do have them, occasionally."

"I didn't mean it like that," she said, and they teetered on the edge again.

"Sorry, I know you didn't," MJ said quickly. "I'm sorry."

"I'm sorry, too." She took a breath. "How is the little girl? Hannah, isn't it?"

"Hannah, yes. She's pretty out of it, which is the best thing for her. It was the parents who really needed me to-night, so we could talk through what's happening with surgery and what the recovery process will be."

"She hasn't had the surgery yet?"

"We need to wait until her condition has stabilized. It might be a few days."

"That's a hard wait, for the parents."

"It is. Nothing we can do."

"Except talk to them."

"Except that, which I'll do whenever they need it."

They talked a little more, and it was nice. Cautiously nice. Oh, they were both being so careful, counting such tiny things as a success—the fact that they were sharing news on how they'd each spent their time, the fact that they didn't yell or close off and that they pulled back from the brink the moment any tension threatened.

The fact that Alicia wasn't faking the interaction, too.

After they'd finished the call and she'd taken the apple bread out of the oven and put it on a rack to cool, she thought she would love the moment when her head hit the pillow, but when it happened, sleep refused to come. She was too churned up over everything.

The way she and MJ had made love last night. The idyllic apple-orchard visit today. His early departure. Her questions about what would happen the next time he came up. Her all-over-the-place plans about deciding exactly where she and the kids would live, whether she would look for a job or study for some kind of qualification, or whether she owed it to MJ to be a full-time mother to his children at least until they started school.

There was something she'd forgotten to consider in this list, too, and she didn't remember it until early Sunday afternoon, when a self-drive moving truck with bright lettering painted on the side pulled into the driveway, followed a minute or two later by a sleek little car.

Andy and Claudia were coming home today, and this was them.

The kids were excited about the truck, as soon as they heard it. They wanted to go outside and see the big vehicle and what was inside it, so Alicia opened the front door and they all came down the porch steps into the front yard. Andy hopped down from the cab and gave each child a fond uncle's greeting, throwing a nice hello to Alicia as he lifted them in turn for a hug and a swing back to the ground.

"You're earlier than I expected." She couldn't quite keep the dismay out of her voice.

How was she going to tell Andy about the separation? *What* was she going to tell him? She'd never planned to pretend about it, once he and Claudia were back. She was going to tell them the truth as soon as she could. But she wasn't totally sure what the truth was anymore. And how did you put any of it into words?

Andy didn't notice her uncomfortable reaction. He was too busy opening up the back of the truck and checking on Claudia's arrival in the car. Yes, she and Ben had pulled safely in right behind him, leaving enough room to unload the truck. They had brought up her remaining possessions from her apartment in New York City, which they'd decided to rent out unfurnished.

"We can wait to unload," he was telling Claudia. "I'll call up Ethan and Chris. They're on standby for the heavy stuff. What time, do you think?"

"Between three and four? Hi, Alicia. Hi, Abby. Hi, Tyler," Claudia said in a quick aside. She and Alicia had only met a couple of times.

"Sounds about right," Andy answered her. "Let's get Ben organized first and bring in some of the easier stuff if we have time before they get here." The baby was nearly six months old and getting incredibly cute, with his brown eyes and toothless smile. More settled, too, after three months or more of not recognizing the meaning of the word *routine*.

"That makes sense," Claudia agreed. She unstrapped Ben from his car seat and loaded herself up with his necessary baby gear, while he sat in the crook of her arm, then headed for the house. Abby and Tyler began to follow her, and she said to Abby, "Honey, could you carry the diaper bag for me?"

Andy turned to Alicia. "I'm glad we caught you. I thought you might have left already,"

"Left?"

"Aren't you heading back today? You said a few days. I didn't think MJ would hold it together without you for much longer than that on his own." He was joking. She could tell by the flip tone.

For some reason it grated on her raw emotional state, because it seemed to imply that the opposite was true— that MJ would "hold it together" without batting an eyelid—and she was goaded into saying very bluntly the words she'd rehearsed the whole drive up from Manhattan on Wednesday. "MJ and I have split up."

The announcement fell between them as if someone had thrown a brick.

Split up.

MJ and I have split up.

Andy looked at her, with the brick sitting on the ground between them.

He was MJ's brother, but they didn't look that much alike. Andy's features were less even, he had a distinctly crooked nose, a squarer jaw and he wasn't quite as dark or as tall as MJ. Still, the McKinley resemblance was there, and right now she was incredibly aware of it.

She'd just told MJ's brother that she'd left her marriage.

"Right," he said after a moment. He stood there.

"I didn't want to tell you on the phone." She folded her hands tightly together in an effort to get them to keep still.

"No, that's okay. Of course you didn't."

"I wanted to tell you in person." Oh, but she shouldn't have told him at all! Not yet! "Thank you for letting me use your place. If you feel I have it under false pretenses…"

"No. Don't be stupid. You needed somewhere to go. For the children's sake, especially."

"Yes, that was a big reason for my choosing your place. It made things—" how could she phrase it? "—more normal."

"You know I love having the kids up here," he said neutrally.

She took a steadying breath and asked the big favor, the one that had suddenly become important now that someone else knew what was going on. "Would you mind... not mentioning it to anyone just yet?"

"Of course I won't," he answered in a guarded way. "If that's what you want."

"Not even Claudia," she continued quickly, before she could lose courage on this. She'd planned on telling Claudia, too, but for some reason she couldn't stand the idea of Andy's fiancée knowing about it right now, when there were still so many questions. "If it's fair of me to ask that."

"I can manage," he drawled.

"MJ and I have a lot still to work out. I'd rather we'd had a chance to do that before...well, before we have to deal with people's reactions."

"Of course," Andy said again, totally courteous and polite about it. "I understand that. And in fact, it's probably for the best. But I'm not sure how long you'll have that luxury."

Her attention caught on the word *luxury*. Was time to think and plan a luxury?

But Andy was still speaking. "I have some news, too, you see. Claudia and I have changed the plans for our wedding. We're not getting married in the city now. We're getting married up here."

"Here? When?"

"Same date as before. Two weeks from yesterday."

"Here," she echoed blankly. It wasn't good news from her point of view. It would put the decisions she needed to make, and the contact and talking that MJ wanted, under so much more pressure.

"We realized we didn't want city hall. We wanted a church. And we wanted to be married in the place where we're making our future."

"That…makes sense."

"It's still going to be small, as we always intended, just a restaurant dinner afterward for family and friends. But yeah, everyone will be here. I assume you don't have plans for being in a place of your own that soon."

"No, not really. I—I have more thinking to do." Especially since yesterday and Friday night.

There was a painful silence. Andy was still looking at her, and she had to fight not to come out with a gabble of words that he didn't need to hear—her half-formed plans for the future, her justifications, her doubts, MJ's plea that they give their marriage more of a chance.

But as she stood there, wondering what more she could say, since it obviously wasn't a good idea to let loose with any of that, she realized two things.

Andy wasn't surprised about the split.

And he wasn't sorry.

Chapter Eleven

"MJ."

"Andy." MJ already knew what this Sunday-evening call from his younger brother was about.

Well, what else could it be about?

"Listen…" Andy said.

MJ cut to the chase. "She told you." He was due back at the hospital, after snatching a half hour at home to shower and shave. He badly needed a haircut. He hated when it began to flop over his eyes. He must manage to squeeze one in this week. Why was he thinking about it now? It was so trivial, yet it provided a nagging counterpoint to the emotional earthquake in his life.

"Yes, she did," Andy was saying. "Who else knows, can I ask?"

"No one. Or at least…" Hell, he hadn't even thought about it! Had she told her friends? Maybe they'd been in on every bit of her thinking and planning for months. Cheering from the sidelines. Helping out with ideas.

That cut.

But her friends weren't the people Andy meant. "So, Mom and Dad, Scarlett and Daniel…? Alicia said she doesn't want them knowing yet, but I wondered if you felt the same or if—"

"I haven't told them, and I'm hoping I won't have to." He'd had three hours' sleep in his own bed last night and another hour in one of the doctor's on-call rooms at the hospital. In addition to the time and attention Hannah Majeska needed, two serious—and surgically challenging—trauma cases had come in. His professional self was glad he'd been there to handle them, yet he ached with the desire to head back north to continue what he and Alicia had started.

"Won't have to?" Andy echoed. "You mean, not yet? Like Alicia said?"

"I mean not at all. Look, we're working through it, talking about what's gone wrong and trying to solve it. I'm feeling very positive. We've already covered a lot of ground."

He stopped and waited for some encouragement from his brother, but it didn't come. The silence at the other end of the phone was awkward. And meaningful.

MJ felt the muscles knot at his temples. He gritted his teeth. "This is not your concern, Andy. My marriage is my business." Then he couldn't help himself. "What has she said?"

"Not much."

"So your judgmental attitude is based on what, exactly?"

"I'm not being—"

"I can read the silence. Either you don't think we *should*

try to work things out, or you don't think we have a snow-ball's chance at it. Which?"

Another beat of silence, then his brother said, "Both."

"Both."

"MJ, it was pretty obvious from the beginning that she married you for what you could—"

"You're wrong."

"I would be very happy to be wrong." The tone said Andy was one-hundred-percent sure that he wasn't.

"Do you have any idea how much you *don't* understand about my marriage? I don't want to talk about this."

"Neither do I, in particular. I just needed to know whether you agreed with Alicia that not even Claudia should know, that's all. I need to know if there's anything you want me to say to anyone. *You,* not Alicia."

"Say nothing. I'm not sure why you're so sure I'll disagree with Alicia on this. There's no need for Claudia or anyone else to know."

"There might be, pretty soon. As I told Alicia, we've changed our wedding plans a little. We're going to do it up here. I thought you might want me to—"

"I don't want you to do anything. Or say anything. We'll deal with the wedding. That's two weeks away." Before Andy could insert his opinion that two weeks wasn't anywhere near long enough for putting a marriage back together, he plowed on. "There's no need for you to give anyone your bull-dust, touchy-feely take on the situation, okay?"

"Try to remember to breathe while you're saying that."

"You push my buttons so damned much, do you know that, Andy?"

"Yeah, and you push mine, so we're even."

At that point, MJ jammed his thumb on his phone to disconnect the call and threw the thing on the bed.

Then picked it up again when it rang four seconds later. "Dr. McKinley?" It was Louise Majeska. "I'm sorry, I'm calling from the unit, and they said—"

"I'm on my way in, Louise. I know you want to talk about the scans. I'm very encouraged, but I want to show you and David exactly what's going on."

He left the apartment in darkness and silence a couple of minutes later.

Alicia looked at the apple upside-down cake on the countertop. It was still faintly warm from the oven, and she'd dusted it with confectionery sugar. To her it looked and smelled like Christmas and Halloween and Grammie's kitchen all rolled into one.

She was proud of it.

And it created a dilemma.

There was too much of it just for herself and the kids. She didn't know when MJ would next be back here.

Or if.

She'd frozen the spiced apple-and-walnut cake she'd made with the hindrance—that is, the *help*—of Abby and Tyler today, but they didn't want her to freeze this one. It had to be dessert.

Andy and Claudia were right next door, and they'd had a tiring day with the drive up from New York and all the unloading, even with the cheerful and rather loud help of Andy's friends, who'd left a couple of hours ago. The obvious solution would be to take the cake across and share it with them, but...

But.

There was a huge, horrible ache inside her because of what she'd seen on Andy's face today. She didn't know which she hated worse—the lack of surprise or the lack of regret.

How could she confront either of those things again?

"But if I don't..." she muttered to herself.

How would that be any better? The awkwardness would only get worse as time went by. She didn't want Andy to know how clearly she'd read him or how much it hurt. She didn't want him to think she was avoiding him.

He thought she'd married MJ for his money. He thought their marriage wasn't worth saving. He thought the split was inevitable, written into the very foundation of their relationship and long overdue.

Was it any wonder she wanted to avoid him?

But she couldn't. She mustn't.

Bite the bullet, Alicia.

"Kids!" she called. They were playing in the front room, the carpet covered in a bright litter of wooden blocks from one of the toy tubs she'd brought up from the city. "We're going next door to Uncle Andy's for dessert."

That got an immediate "Yay!" from Abby, which Tyler soon copied. They left the blocks—the mess would greet Alicia later tonight, once the children were asleep—and tumbled out the front door and along the porch to the adjacent entrance to the main part of the house, while Alicia followed in their wake, bearing her sweet-smelling creation.

It looked to her like a bribe, suddenly, or a cheap ploy.

I've baked. Do gold-digging wives bake?

She hardened her attitude. Didn't understand, actually, why she felt so bad about all of this. After all, wasn't Andy right? Hadn't she married his brother for the worst and most obvious reason in the world? Wasn't that why she'd left MJ—because the deal hadn't proved worth the price?

Abby had already stretched up to ring the bell.

Claudia appeared, wearing slightly grubby jeans and a

pink sweatshirt. She looked tired but content. "Oh, wow! That looks fabulous, Alicia."

"We're hoping you'll share."

"Andy's giving Ben his bath."

"Oh, so do you need to get him to sleep before you can sit and eat?"

"No, he'll be fine for another half hour or so. He'd love to have his cousins for some entertainment, I'm sure."

His cousins.

She almost cried.

Abby and Tyler had a baby cousin now, and she was taking them out of the McKinley family circle. Had Andy told Claudia? He'd said he wouldn't, after she'd asked for that, and there was nothing in the other woman's behavior to suggest otherwise.

But maybe she wouldn't react too strongly to the split, even if she did know. She was very new in the family, so she hadn't had time to develop an opinion on the hot topic of the moment—the state of MJ and Alicia's marriage

Scarlett, on the other hand...

"Scarlett and Dan are coming over to help us unpack," Claudia said cheerfully. Scarlett had begun work as a pediatrician at Spring Ridge Memorial Hospital, and from all accounts was thoroughly happy with her new life in Vermont and her engagement to Daniel Porter. "So this is great timing. I was about to take inventory and see if we possibly had anything to give them for supper." She stopped and did a rapid and very visible rethink. "That is...if you don't mind me making executive decisions on who gets to eat something I had no hand at all in creating. Sorry, did I overstep?"

"Of course you didn't." Did she come across as that selfish? That she would begrudge sharing a *cake?* "There's plenty for Scarlett and Daniel, too."

They arrived just as Andy came back downstairs with a freshly bathed Ben. Alicia automatically reached out her arms for him, as the beam of Scarlett and Daniel's car headlights swung through the room, muted a little by the shrubbery outside. Little Ben smelled so sweet and clean and good, from the silky fine hair at the crown of his head to the stretchy cotton feet of his teddy-bear-patterned sleeper.

What was it about babies? They just felt so right. They—

MJ didn't use protection the other night.

It hit her like a hard gust of wind around a corner, and she couldn't believe it was the first time she'd thought about it, since that passionate session in the kitchen on Friday night. How could they have forgotten?

Well, because you didn't use a bed, remember, Alicia?

They had turned their back on the tired habit of MJ reaching for her when he was already half-asleep, then reaching again to open the drawer of the bedside table. They'd been so caught up in what was happening, and Alicia's doubts had all been about a very different kind of risk than pregnancy—the emotional risk of the physical intimacy.

Before conceiving Abby, she had been on the Pill. She'd gone off it, gotten pregnant at once and hadn't used contraception again until she'd stopped breast-feeding Tyler when he was six months old. She and MJ both knew that a pregnancy was quite possible when you were breast-feeding, but they'd been willing to take the risk—MJ liked the idea of three kids, or even four—and in the end nothing had happened.

Two years of the Pill, three and a half years of nothing at all, eighteen months or so of the little packets in the bedside drawer and the vague idea in both their heads for at least some of those months that another baby might be in the plan. Contraception hadn't been high on her agenda. She was out of the habit.

And yet how could she have forgotten? Since she'd started thinking seriously about ending the marriage, she'd monitored those little packets very carefully. How could she have been so distracted two nights ago?

But, wait a minute, did it matter? What was the timing on this?

She thought for about five seconds.

It mattered.

It was entirely possible.

Claudia opened the door for the new arrivals and greeted Scarlett with a warm hug. There was a bit of a flurry. Daniel shook Andy's hand. Abby hugged Scarlett's knees. Scarlett came over and gave Alicia an air kiss and they touched each other's shoulders in a stiff, brief way, with Ben looking on from the crook of Alicia's arm.

She felt as if she wasn't really here.

Had never really been here, in this family.

She suddenly ached desperately for MJ to be standing beside her, because at least he gave her some validation. That ring on her finger. They were *married,* which meant that no matter what anyone else thought, she had the right to hold her head up; she had the right to some respect. Gold digger or not, she wasn't a mistress. She was a wife.

And now she was throwing all of that away.

Throwing her life with MJ away.

Even though she loved him down to her bones.

A wave of shock ran through her.

This was a revelation, far more shocking than remembering Friday night's lack of contraception.

She loved MJ.

She *loved* him.

This was why their marriage wasn't working. Not because she *didn't* love him but because she *did*. He gave her so little of himself, and she was so angry about it, angry with herself as well as with him—had been angry about it for so long that it masked and sullied the love completely— but if she hadn't loved him, his absence wouldn't have mattered. The love and the anger had grown in strength and depth and power together, from the very beginning.

She'd left her marriage not because she didn't care but because it was hurting too much for her to stay, with the way MJ took her for granted and with her own artificial behavior. She loved him, and she was angry, and he didn't even know who she was, and whose fault was that?

"Are you okay, Alicia?" Scarlett asked.

"Can you take the baby?"

"Of course."

"I'm fine. Really. Just felt a little faint."

"Do you want to sit down?"

I want to curl up in bed and die.

"Maybe I should," she agreed.

Andy took the baby and Scarlett led Alicia to the couch, showing some of the warmth she hadn't shown when they hugged. Alicia felt stupidly needy about it.

They were sisters-in-law. They should care about each other.

The combination of Andy clearly not caring all that much about the breakdown of his brother's marriage and Scarlett clearly not caring all that much about *her* made Alicia feel three times more of a failure than she already was.

She hadn't realized how the whole McKinley family felt. She'd been so caught up in playing the role of good trophy wife, it hadn't occurred to her that they might see through the pretense, see the full ugliness of the marital bargain she and MJ had made.

Oh, she wanted him here so much! There was a hard ball of distress lodged in her throat and she was fighting tears, and it was so *weird* that she suddenly felt as if she and MJ were allies in this when she'd been feeling so distant from him for so long.

The family attitude was a condemnation of both of them, that was the thing.

MJ didn't come out of this looking any better than she did.

"Are you sure you're okay, Alicia?"

"I will be. In a bit."

She wanted to flee next door to the privacy and quiet and call him. Just to hear his voice. To hear if he was still trying as hard as he'd tried yesterday and last night, or if his surge of willingness would prove shallow and brief and would already have worn off. The fear of this possibility gnawed at her.

Maybe he would start thinking more deeply and clearly. Maybe his knee-jerk reaction of fighting this purely because it wasn't his own idea would wear off. He was so accustomed to calling the shots, but he would at some point get over the fact that he hadn't been the first one to act, and at this point he would surely conclude that divorce was the best thing for him.

He could afford to pay generous alimony to support her and the children without compromising his own lifestyle. He must know that she wouldn't block his access to Abby and Tyler. Any limitations on that wouldn't be made by her but by him. He could see them as much as his own demanding schedule allowed. Even if he did expect a custody battle, he had the resources to fight it. He could marry again, someone far more suitable for the long haul this time around. He could be happy.

For all she knew—and it killed her to think it—he might already have someone else waiting in the wings. A mistress, biding her time through snatched lunchtime meetings. A colleague who wasn't above pursuing a married man and who might be well aware of how little time MJ spent with his wife.

No. *No.* Alicia had no reason to question MJ's fidelity or to suspect another woman lying in wait. She remembered how much agony there'd been in his voice the other night when he'd asked her if there was someone else. But the idea haunted her all the same—if not in the present, then in the future.

"Whoa-ho, this looks *great!*" Andy said.

Claudia had come into the room, carrying a tray bearing a tub of ice cream, bowls and spoons, and Alicia's apple cake cut into eight generous triangular slices.

Alicia had to blink back tears at Andy's praise, thankful that the activity of serving the dessert distracted any attention from her emotion. It shocked her that she was this needy. To come so close to losing control purely because of some positive words from Andy about her cooking, when he'd seemed so cool about the prospect of her divorce.

Oh, but Andy's words were just the trigger, not the heart of it. She had plenty of better reasons to cry.

"Yum, Alicia," said Scarlett, while the kids reached for theirs and Tyler had to be persuaded to use his spoon instead of his fingers.

Alicia recognized that she'd done a good job with the recipe, but still the cake tasted to her like cardboard and glue, and if faking orgasms and faking having fun with your kids were hard, then faking cheerful social interaction with her brother-in-law and sister-in-law and their partners was even harder. Her mind was whirling.

She loved MJ, and a part of her could so easily have thrown the kids into the car and driven down to the city right now to tell him, "I'm sorry. I don't want a divorce. I need you in my life too much."

But if she gave in and returned to her marriage, things would be back the way they were within a week. She would fall back into faking her perfect performance, and MJ wouldn't even notice. He would relax as soon as the threat of divorce went away. All that will to win would be channeled right back into his work and his success, and he would soon forget that these few days of turmoil had ever happened.

Worse, he would be even less inclined to take her seriously in the future. Why listen to a wife who threatened divorce and changed her mind less than a week later?

Yes, she loved MJ, but she was still deeply angry at him.

It was no news to her that love and anger could co-exist like this. She and Grammie had both been angry at Mom for the whole five years they were together, and yet they'd loved her and missed her and grieved over her death so much.

Alicia's earliest memories were of those two emotions mixed.

Love and anger.

She remembered tenderly kissing her mother's cheek one morning—she must only have been around four years old—and then hitting her furiously with a pillow because she smelled and she mumbled and swore and she wouldn't wake up enough to make breakfast, and all Alicia had been able to find in the kitchen was instant coffee and a half-empty packet of peanuts. "Mommy, c'mon, I'm *hungry*."

Love and anger.

They were an incredibly potent combination.

Incredibly painful, too.

She knew it would be the worst mistake she'd ever made if she went back to MJ now.

She fought her way through the evening, hiding behind her interactions with Abby and Tyler when she needed to, fighting to show the right enthusiasm for Andy and Claudia's wedding plans, which they were both buzzing about, following the change of venue.

"Thinking back, city hall in Manhattan was just never right. We decided on that originally so that people wouldn't have to travel."

"But then Len and Dorie let slip that they weren't looking forward to a splashy Manhattan dinner, so we pulled the whole plan apart and worked out what we really wanted."

"Not the whole plan," Claudia said. "The essence is the same. We want it simple and romantic and fun and small, because if we try for something too huge and complicated, I'll get all uptight and start printing out schedules timed down to thirty seconds. Andy already had to ban me from reading bride magazines."

"Simple and romantic and fun and small. We're thinking along those lines, too," Scarlett said about her own wedding plans. She and Daniel were so relaxed they weren't talking dates or venues or anything. "We might take ourselves by surprise. You watch. We'll go away for a weekend in Paris sometime next spring and come back married." She grinned. "Or we'll do it while skydiving."

"Didn't MJ and Alicia already do the surprise-wedding trick in Las Vegas?" Daniel asked.

Alicia caught a glance from Andy that he quickly tried to hide. Yeah...no, just seeing if he should collect the empty dessert plates. Not instinctively checking out

Alicia's reaction to the Las Vegas wedding thing at all, oh, no, sirree.

He'd obviously honored Alicia's request not to tell anyone about her and MJ's news, but it was going to be difficult to ask for his silence for much longer, especially with the whole family coming up here for a wedding in less than two weeks.

And yet she needed it. She and MJ desperately needed more time and no family breathing down their necks trying to understand what was going on.

When we don't understand what's going on, ourselves.

She followed Andy into the kitchen with Abby and Tyler's sticky plates and loaded them into the dishwasher when he stood back to let her do so. "Thank you, Andy. You haven't said anything…"

"Not a word."

"…and I appreciate that. I—I think MJ would, too."

"I know he would, because he said so." He loaded his own small pile of empty dessert plates into the machine.

"You've talked to him?" She was shocked.

"I called him."

"To hear his side of the story," she guessed.

"He is my brother." He straightened and closed the dishwasher. "I think that's reasonable, don't you?" They stood facing each other, and Andy took a step back and reached for a cleaning sponge from the sink—not because he planned on wiping down any surfaces but as a way of increasing the distance.

"Yes, I guess," Alicia answered him. "I hope it was a reasonable conversation. MJ and I are both trying for that. Courtesy. And kindness."

"Actually, kindness is better than MJ and I managed to each other," Andy said abruptly. It sounded like a confession.

"What do you mean?"

"We got under each other's skin. Nothing new. We always have."

"Why are you telling me this, Andy? Any of this?"

"I think I was unfair to you, before, and I think you picked up on it. I have no right to judge. MJ seems pretty convinced that the two of you will work things out." He added in a wooden tone, "It would be great if you did."

"You think?" she asked lightly, and he had the grace to look uncomfortable.

"What I think doesn't matter," he said.

No, maybe not. Maybe none of what any of the McKinleys thought, barring MJ himself, mattered in the slightest. And yet Alicia knew the undercurrent of skepticism about their marriage had affected her over the years, made their already shaky bargain that much worse.

"I'll try to remember that," she told Andy, and even though the words had an edge, the criticism lying behind them was directed mainly at herself.

Chapter Twelve

"Please come up again as soon as you can," Alicia had said to MJ on the phone on Sunday night. "We need to get this sorted out, one way or the other."

She'd sounded strained and unhappy, and the darkest part of him had thought, *Good. If this is no picnic for you, Alicia, that's only what you deserve.* The better part of him had hated to hear her struggling so much, pretending things were fine, giving the truth away only in her tone and that one plea.

Now it was Thursday afternoon and he was doing as she'd asked. Hannah Majeska had been through her epic session of surgery, with himself and two other orthopedic specialists working over her for eleven solid hours. The other two trauma cases he had covered the worst and then turned over to his juniors for the next forty-eight hours, and there was *nothing* important enough in the world of medicine to bring him back to the city this time, before those forty-eight hours were over.

He thought about telling Alicia exactly how much effort it had taken to shift his schedule around and off-load his cases and appointments. Fifteen phone calls, and that didn't include the ones his office staff would have to make. Even in his head, though, he could hear how arrogant it would sound, and saying it out loud would be worse.

He'd never questioned his own ego before. Dad considered it a vital tool in a doctor's skill set and he agreed. If you doubted yourself, you would never have the courage to go into the O.R. with guns blazing and stop someone's heart, or transplant their liver, or fill them with plates and screws.

But maybe you had to learn to keep your ego purely for the job. Maybe your personal life was different, and you had to be more humble there.

Lord, he felt he'd had more lessons in humility these past eight days than he'd had in his whole life.

"Maybe I need them," he said to the ribbon of road spooling out beneath his wheels.

He drove through without stopping, because he was too impatient to lose a moment, and arrived on the outskirts of Radford at just after four.

MJ had texted Alicia with his arrival time as he left the city. He'd updated his estimate twice when he hit traffic and realized he was going to be a little later than he'd first said, and she knew his precision about the time was yet another signal that he was trying hard.

But it left her knowing exactly when to expect him, which meant she had so much conflicting emotion pinned on the moment.

Today had passed so slowly, as had the whole six days

since MJ had left. She hadn't seen another adult all day. Andy had been at work, while Claudia had taken little Ben with her on a tour of available office space in the area, as she was hoping to set up her accountancy and financial-planning business within the next few months.

Playing with the children and marshaling them through their daily routine, Alicia had far too much time to think, and the thoughts were repetitive and unproductive.

What if she was pregnant? Would that be the solution to everything or the worst thing that could happen? An omen or a trap? A blessing or a curse? Would she tell MJ about the possibility or wait and see? It would be crazy to tell him, when there was only a chance. Did it change anything, anyhow?

Maybe even the fact that she kept thinking about it was a destructive distraction from more important questions. She loved him, but love was only a part of the answer.

She had wanted to take the kids to a pumpkin-picking place, following the success of apple picking last week, but when she'd mentioned that to MJ on the phone last night, he'd vetoed it. "Save that for Friday. The apple orchard was so nice. Don't shut me out."

"I'm not trying to shut you out."

"No, okay. But save it? Could you?"

"Sure, yes. You're right, it would be nice to go as a family."

But it left her plans for today far too light—just a morning visit to a nearby playground that they hadn't yet explored; some indoor play; and a lunch of crackers and cheese, dips, and carrot and red-pepper sticks to put in the dips. It was quite a good lunch for passing a little extra time. Tyler wiped his carrot sticks through the dip with his father's surgical precision but managed to get into a mess anyhow.

She'd tried to put him down for his nap at one, but he was still way too wakeful and energetic at that stage and hadn't settled until almost two-thirty, which meant he was still asleep now, at five after four, and wouldn't be ready for bed tonight until after nine.

Disastrously, Abby had fallen asleep, too, in front of the DVD Alicia had put on to entertain her while she was putting Tyler down. Abby's nap had probably only lasted half an hour, but that would be enough to put back her bedtime schedule, as well.

Meanwhile, MJ would be here at any moment, and she had no idea how their interaction over the next day or two would pan out.

Abby wanted to sit on the porch swing and watch for Daddy, so here they were, the two of them, sitting and swinging, while Alicia's stomach fluttered. This was his car now, slowing and turning into the driveway. Abby slid from the swing, making it rock unevenly, and raced down the steps, shrieking, "Daddy!"

She was always so excited about seeing her father. What did that say? That MJ was a great father? Or that Abby was unhealthily needy because she saw him so rarely? Worse, was Abby echoing a neediness she'd unconsciously picked up in Alicia herself?

Alicia followed her daughter out to the car more slowly, trying to get a grip on herself, willing her pulse to slow and her breathing to steady.

This was crazy.

This tall, well-built man with the sunglasses shading his eyes was the husband she was leaving, the man who'd made anger settle so deeply into her bones that it felt like a heavy metal, full of toxic radiation, and a permanent part of her.

But she loved him so much. She knew she was to blame,

too, for all that had gone wrong between them, and he was trying so hard. All she wanted was to fling herself into his arms as Abby was doing right now, and feel his body against hers and tell him, *It was all a mistake. I can't live without you.*

Oh, and she so nearly did it. Seeing the smooth shape of his head revealed by a fresh haircut since the weekend and the fine lines of fatigue around his eyes when he took off his sunglasses and slid them into a pocket. Seeing him come so cautiously toward her, with Abby perched on his hip. Seeing the uncertainty written on his face. Feeling the tiny, unknowable possibility of his baby growing inside her again.

He didn't know how to greet her, she realized. Should he smile? Should he kiss her?

She wanted to signal a very powerful answer to those unspoken questions.

Please kiss me. Please take me in your arms.

But then the old Alicia—the scared, cynical, solitary Alicia—took hold of her limbs and froze them in place. *Keep him guessing, girlfriend. It's the only power you have. If you give too much, he'll trample on your heart. He'll take you for granted, and nothing will change.*

"Hi," she said finally and hoped to heaven that he hadn't heard the wobble in her voice.

"Hi." He stopped on the stone-flagged path, several yards away. She could see the tension in his shoulders.

"Tyler's still asleep." She stopped, too.

"So, a late bedtime for him tonight, right? For them both, probably."

"I'm afraid so." Her gaze met his, and both were laden with so much subtext that she half expected to hear a sizzle. His eyes dropped to her mouth, and she could feel the pressure and heat of his kiss so powerfully in her imagination. His gaze dropped lower and he stripped her with his eyes and it bathed her in heat and she liked it.

Were they sleeping together tonight, then? Well, not *sleeping*...

Oh, shoot, this was crazy! It was like a second or third date more than a marriage in trouble. The jittery feeling of not knowing who wanted what and what any of it meant.

"Kiss her!" Abby suddenly ordered from her privileged position in MJ's arms. What had she heard and seen in their interaction? What did she suspect?

"You want me to kiss Mommy?" MJ queried, clearly buying time.

"Yes." Abby was incredibly certain about the whole thing. "Kissing is part of saying hi when people love each other." Did she suspect? Even at preschool age, she already had a couple of friends with divorced parents and blended families, including Anna and James's daughter, Elise, currently being fought over like a piece of meat between two dogs. Did Abby have some kind of radar that told her this wasn't the fun fall vacation Mommy and Daddy kept pretending it was?

"That's true." MJ lowered his daughter carefully to the ground and she stood there like a Hollywood director, ready to intervene and reshoot the whole scene if the actors didn't get their performance right the first time.

He stepped closer, and Alicia came to meet him. They didn't hold each other, not even the touch of a hand. He just bent down a little, while she stretched her face up, and their mouths met, soft and sweet and brief, brushing together and then letting go. The warmth of a kiss, the taste of a kiss, but over far too soon. She could have done with so much more.

The director, however, was quite satisfied. "That's

right," she said. "Now let's go in." She marched to the steps.

"I'll get my bag," MJ muttered, turning back to the car, and Alicia didn't know whether to follow Abby or wait for him. Her legs made the decision, refusing to move until he came up beside her with the bag strap slung over his shoulder and the bag itself making his suit jacket pull crookedly open.

"You came straight from patient appointments," Alicia said, registering the way he was dressed and how much of a hurry he must have been in, since he hadn't even removed the jacket.

"If I'd called in at the hospital, I wouldn't have gotten away for another two hours."

But she knew how tempted he must have been. He always called in at the hospital. They'd almost missed flights, in the past, or hit peak-hour traffic, because he'd called in at the hospital last thing before leaving the city, and then the hospital had wrapped its octopus tentacles around him and refused to let him go. He liked the fact that the hospital was so hungry for him.

"I'm glad you didn't, then," she said lightly, and he looked at her and that sizzle appeared in his eyes again, and she couldn't help sending it back to him in full measure. The old Alicia thought, *I'm blowing this. I'm showing my hand too soon.* The new Alicia had a different way of ending the sentence. *I'm showing my heart too nakedly.*

But it amounted to the same thing. She stifled her need to touch him and kept her hand pinned at her side. She didn't want him to think he'd won yet, because he hadn't. She couldn't live with the anger and the love anymore, and if she couldn't get rid of the anger, then it would have to be the love that she learned to go without.

The children dominated the next five hours. Tyler

awoke grumpy and distressed after his nap, which he often did these days if it had started too late and gone on too long. Again, Alicia faced the fact that he would be giving it up soon, and she didn't know whether to force the issue now or wait a little longer. Would MJ possibly be interested in a discussion of the pros and cons?

She put the question on the back burner—something she could try talking about to him if they had some private time and were stuck for conversation.

Abby was like a bulldozer in her need for parental attention, and again Alicia wondered how much a four-year-old could suspect. The Hollywood director persona came to the fore again. "Mommy, sit here, and Daddy, sit here." And a little later, "Daddy, what's your favorite dinner? Because Mommy is going to make it tonight."

"Oh, I am?" Alicia said.

"My favorite dinner is take-out pizza," MJ said firmly, and the two adults shared a private smile that zinged right over Abby's head.

Oh, that was nice! If they could just find more moments like that!

So they had take-out pizza, and the kids gobbled theirs down and were ready for a DVD in the front room, while Alicia and MJ were still taking it slowly at the kitchen table, with salad on the side and glasses of red wine. It would probably be the only private time they managed tonight.

Or at least until the kids were asleep. After that…

After that was a little scary to think about. They were going to make love again. Alicia knew it and wanted it—wanted it quite fiercely—but sex with or without protection wouldn't solve anything on its own, no matter how much it echoed the physical passion of their first year together.

"Can we play the game?" she asked, suddenly desperate to make something out of this private time in the kitchen, for the sake of what later tonight might come to mean.

"The—?" Then MJ remembered. "The 'three things' game."

"Yes." She said the first thing she could think of, didn't want to spend too long on it, because it was…might be… just a silly game that meant nothing. "Three of your favorite movies, the first ones that come into your head."

"Um, okay, *Raiders of the Lost Ark, You Only Live Twice* and *Groundhog Day*. Yours?"

"Well, can I recover from the astonishment at yours first?"

"Not so astonishing, do you think? Obviously I wanted to be Indiana Jones and James Bond. Preferably both at the same time. *Groundhog Day* hit me because it wasn't meant to make me think, but it did."

"About what?"

He spoke slowly. "Oh, mortality and choices, and how we deal with the fact that life can be lived so many different ways."

"Remind me to see that movie again sometime." She'd seen it on cable more than once but not while MJ was there. In fact, she'd seen all three of his movies but none of them with him.

"Now three of yours," he said, before she was ready. "Top of your head. I wasn't allowed to think about it, and neither are you."

"Right, okay…*Big Business, Sense and Sensibility* and the first Harry Potter."

"I haven't even heard of *Big Business*…"

"Oh, it was this silly little movie from the eighties with Bette Midler and Lily Tomlin." She felt almost apologetic about her choice but then remembered the night she'd watched it. "And I caught it on cable a couple of years ago, and I always love both those actresses, and I laughed till I cried."

She thought of what else she could say about watching the movie that night. Should she say it? She hadn't realized when it came into her head that her feelings about it were so loaded. Laughed till she cried but could have cut to the chase and left out the laughing part. Just kept the tears.

"Can I say…?" she began slowly.

"Say anything."

Disney came from the other room. She knew both kids were there, and safe, because Abby complained suddenly, in a voice that was pure American, not County Cork at all, "Tyler, you're sitting on my foot."

"I think it might spoil the game," Alicia said.

"The game has a point, Alicia." He straightened, took a mouthful of wine and looked at her more closely. "It's not just a game, and you know it. If we're getting down to something here, then say it."

"I sat there watching it all by myself, because you were at the hospital, and Tyler was only a week old—" *am I pregnant again?* "—and I was so sore and tired, and we had that nanny I really didn't like— Shoot, I've blanked out on her name."

"Robyn. The Australian girl with the weird hair."

"Her." She was actually pleased he'd remembered. Robyn had only been with them a couple of months. It proved he took some notice, at least. "I was letting her go out whenever she asked because I didn't want her around, and she'd begun to take advantage of that and went out almost every night. She was useless when she was out and horrible when she was around, but I didn't want to bite the bullet and fire her, because we might not find anyone better right away, and then I'd be stuck with an even worse nanny, or no nanny at all, and a newborn and Abby—who was a *nightmare* for the first six months after Tyler was born."

"And I was *never there*." There was an edge. He was quoting. From the note she'd left for him last week.

"Well, you weren't. And when you were…"

"When I was, you *never talked*." He was mocking both of them, there. "So how could I know you were feeling like that?"

"So you're saying it's my fault? That if I'd communicated better, you would have started coming home at six and not working weekends?"

"I'm a senior surgeon. I can't do that."

"You're doing it now."

"This is an extremely short-term situation, Alicia."

"Oh, my threatened walkout is short-term?"

"No. *No!*" His hand tightened into a fist and he almost thumped the table with it but paused just in time. The kids would have heard. "My ability to spend this time is short-term. I'm doing it because it's important. Vital."

His voice cracked suddenly, and so did her anger. Cracked and fell apart like a broken, flower-filled vase, so that her love flooded out in a mess of water and stems—oh, like that made sense!—and she listened to him helplessly as she fought for control.

"It can't last too long," he said quietly. "I'm sorry, but it just can't. Would you really ask me to compromise the work I love? The work I'm made for? You married me knowing the kinds of hours I needed to work. You knew the deal going in."

The deal changed, she wanted to tell him. *It changed when I fell in love with you, and that happened so gradually I didn't see it. It happened right along with the anger, and now I'm stuck and I don't know what to do.*

But he was still speaking. "Long-term, I can cut down my hours a little, if it would help. Would it help?"

"I—I think so."

"Tell me exactly what you want."

I want you to say you love me and that you'd crawl over broken glass. I want another baby with you.

"In terms of hours," he added.

She dragged herself onto that rational, careful marital level and tried not to ask for the moon and stars. "Could you manage twice a week to come home before the kids are asleep? Could we turn the TV off while you eat, even when you're tired, so we can talk? And could there be half a day every weekend when we do something as a family?"

"Does it have to be the same two evenings and the same half day each week?"

"N-no, it can float. It can be last-minute."

"That would be easier."

"It can't be put off and off so that it never actually happens."

"Sometimes it might have to be put off."

"Sometimes. Not often. That's where I get to the point where I'd rather not have you at all."

"The point you're at now."

"Yes."

"Yes. So it's still yes. Still yes, we're getting a divorce." He stopped and swore, and she understood why. Once again, he'd pushed for a quick answer, when she'd asked him not to, and now he was beating himself up for his own impatience and for forgetting her request, and her heart went out to him and she came so close to giving him what he wanted.

I'll come back to the city. I love you. Just tell me you love me and I don't care about anything else.

But that last part wasn't true. She did care about other

things. She'd had love for a while—on her side at least, even though she hadn't fully realized it—and the anger that came with it told her love wasn't enough.

"And to think, this started with three of our favorite movies," she tried to joke, instead of coming out with that loaded *L* word.

The humor was wobbly, but it seemed to help and he followed her lead. "Yeah, we might be in real trouble if we go for the really strong stuff. Three favorite books. Three favorite tropical islands."

"I really liked Martinique," she put in slyly, but already he'd thrown the lightness away.

"Alicia…" He leaned in and pressed his forehead against hers. "I'm sorry that you've felt abandoned and alone. I never intended that."

"What did you intend?"

"A partnership, remember? Obviously it needs to be more equal. I will try. We'll sit down every week with our schedules and make sure to put in the right blocks of time." He spoke with his usual confidence, made it sound so efficient and easy.

Alicia remembered the team-building meetings that Tony Cottini would occasionally throw at them at the restaurant seven years ago. They all had to sit in an arc around a whiteboard offering "carrots," things they were happy with, and "sticks," things they wanted to change, and the meetings would end with a series of "action points."

She remembered one that had come from one of her "sticks." *Change the napkin dispensers,* Tony had scribbled on the whiteboard with great enthusiasm, under the "action points" heading, but several months later, when she came back from Las Vegas with MJ's ring on her finger and told Tony she was quitting, the same ancient dispensers were still on the tables and still causing frustrated diners to pull out wads of twenty or thirty at once.

Now MJ seemed to be reducing their marriage to a series of action points, and she wondered whether the end result would be the same as it had been at Tony's—vast enthusiasm in theory but no actual change.

"Blocks of time would help," she said.

"Okay, so that's a start."

"And I know there are changes I need to make, too."

"Yeah?" he said softly. "You seem pretty good to me…."

"I need to be more honest. I need to stop trying to be your idea of perfect all the time."

They both heard the music that signaled the end of Abby and Tyler's DVD and knew that this particular team-building session was over. With the scrambling movement of little bodies already audible from the front room, MJ said in frustration, "This would be a lot easier if Maura was still here. I'm sure we could find someone here in Radford who'd jump at the job."

"I don't want another nanny. Not here. Not yet."

Abby and Tyler both hurtled into the room and zeroed in on the two pizza boxes still on the table. There were several pieces left. "Can I have another one?" Abby asked.

"C'n I, too?" said her little echo.

MJ ignored them both. "Why not? Wouldn't it help? I hate that we've had to cut this talk off before it was finished."

Alicia passed out the slices of pizza and tried to explain in a way that wouldn't prick Abby's very active curiosity. "Lack of privacy of a different kind. I don't want adult ears. Or adult judgment. This is us, MJ. Just us."

"Makes it harder when we have to stop in the middle of something. Impractical. There's more to say."

"Yes. It's not practical. It's not efficient. I'm sorry. I can't—" she made a gesture with her hand and MJ had to fill in the words she hadn't spoken—*heal our marriage* "—efficiently."

She stood up, her body tense and tingling. Here was her old friend anger again. They couldn't outsource the solutions to their problems. They couldn't mask them behind a busy crowd of support staff. They couldn't afford an outsider around, forcing them to pretend for half the time that they were together. They needed everything as simple as possible and they needed to take some serious time, and if MJ still couldn't see that, after all they'd said to each other…

"When pizza's finished, it's bath time," she announced to Abby and Tyler. "And then story, and then bed."

"Which story?" Abby wanted to know. "Can Daddy read it?"

"Yes, Daddy can read it," MJ said.

Family time and bedtime swamped them both for the next hour.

Chapter Thirteen

"Mommy, we can't get to sleep," Abby announced from the top of the stairs.

Alicia heard MJ say a few words under his breath that he probably didn't want his daughter learning for another ten or twelve years, or adding to her own vocabulary ever. To Alicia, he said, although not much louder, "I thought they were down for the count."

She resisted the temptation to tell him, *I could have told you they weren't.*

It was only ten to nine. Both kids had been tucked up at eight-thirty, on MJ's cheerful but very firm insistence, but the way Tyler had wriggled his legs and the liveliness of Abby's tuck-in conversation had signaled to Alicia that there could be problems ahead. She wasn't surprised, after the sleep each child had had in the afternoon.

In the twenty minutes since the optimistic bedtime, she and MJ had finished the wine still in their glasses and looked at pumpkin-picking places on the internet, on MJ's laptop, for tomorrow's planned visit. The weather forecast wasn't great—rain developing for the afternoon, cold all day—but MJ stubbornly insisted that they would dress appropriately and everything would be fine.

Alicia wasn't so sure. MJ was willing them to have as good a day as they'd had last week, but sheer will didn't work with kids. There were too many factors beyond their own control. MJ just wasn't accustomed to that.

"Close your eyes and imagine yourself floating down the most beautiful river," she suggested brightly to Abby. "And all the trees on the riverbank have jewels and gifts in them, and all the birds can talk."

"Tyler keeps talking to me."

"Honey, just ignore him," MJ said. "And then he'll stop and you'll both get sleepy."

"O-kay," she said reluctantly. "Can the beautiful river be made of chocolate?"

"It can be made of anything you want," Alicia told her.

But the chocolate river didn't work. Well, to be fair to the poor thing, it didn't have time. Abby appeared again less than five minutes later. "Tyler won't stop talking to me."

"I'll go up," Alicia said to MJ.

"Isn't that just going to encourage them?"

"I don't think they're doing this on purpose. They both had naps. Don't you hate it when you're too awake to fall asleep?"

"I can always fall asleep," MJ said. "In fact, I'm pretty tired right now." He looked at her, his gaze flicking down her body and up again, with a heat that made her pulses quicken. "Meet you in bed?"

Well, yes, eventually, but what was the intent of the rendezvous? What did she want? When he'd first arrived today, she'd been so hungry for him, as fluttery and un-certain and sensitized as a fairy-tale princess waiting for the first kiss from her one true love. She'd been certain and eager about their lovemaking.

But that feeling had gone, overlaid and suffocated by everything else, by the distance still between them, by all the things he didn't understand.

The things *she* didn't understand, too.

She nodded. "Yes. When I can get there." And didn't know what she was promising. Would they use protection? Would he think of it this time?

"Can you sing songs?" Abby asked as she snuggled back into her bed, with Tyler watching her, bright-eyed and sitting up, in his own bed.

From experience—much of it the nanny's—Alicia knew that singing was the best way to settle them. "Only when you're lying down with your eyes closed, Tyler."

He obediently wriggled down and put his head on the pillow.

Twelve songs later…

Were they really asleep, at last? She tiptoed silently toward the door, barely daring to breathe. It wouldn't be the first time she'd sighed with relief too soon, only to be summoned back by a merciless little voice. *"I'm not asleep yet, Mommy."*

But this time there was nothing. She peeked at them one final time through the last few inches of open door before she eased it shut. Two sets of closed eyes, two little chests rising and falling evenly. They really were asleep.

And so was MJ.

She arrived in their bedroom and knew it right away. There was a heavy quality to his body in the bed, and his breathing was deep. He didn't stir at the sound of her foot-steps or the click of the door.

Oh, the crazy, illogical mix of emotions!

Anger and disappointment, aching love, heartfelt relief and a weird need to laugh.

All through sitting on Abby's bed and singing, she'd been thinking about this moment, imagining MJ waiting for her, pulling her into his arms as soon as she climbed into bed, telling her how much he ached for her.

How much he loved her.

But he never said that.

She'd planned the whole gamut of responses, from pushing him away and sliding to the very edge of her side of the bed, to kissing him hungrily, to doing what she'd done so many times before.

Faking it.

So that it would be over faster and wouldn't actually touch her heart.

No, Alicia, not that.

Standing there, looking at the dim shape of MJ's body beneath the comforter and the dark outline of his fresh haircut on the pillow, she made a vow to herself and to him. She was never going to fake it again.

If she couldn't be honest when she and MJ made love, then their marriage didn't have a chance. And right now, she wanted that chance so badly it almost brought her to tears. She wanted MJ's body. She wanted his heart. She wanted the safety and honesty of darkness, because maybe they would discover something or solve something if they made love in the right, perfect way.

She didn't try especially hard to be quiet as she made her preparations for bed, stepping out again to the bathroom, running the faucet to brush her teeth and take off her makeup, stepping back into the bedroom to open a drawer and pull out the strappy silk-and-lace nightgown that someone—Scarlett, she thought—had given her last Christmas.

That's right, and Scarlett had given MJ a pair of luxurious silk pajamas, which he'd liked so much that he'd commissioned Alicia to buy him a second pair.

She slid into the bed.

He wasn't wearing them.

He wasn't wearing anything.

And he didn't wake up.

Her arm brushed against his back and her knee against his thigh, and they told her what the pulled-up sheet and comforter had hidden. No pajamas. Just skin. She lay there for a moment without touching him, wondering whether to nestle closer. Would her body waken him, when the noise of her movements hadn't? Did she want it to?

This was her chance to pull back from tonight's interactions. Would she take it? She lay there, soothed by the rhythm of his breathing yet totally at a loss about what she wanted. Would he think he'd won if she woke him up with her touch? Did they need to make love again, to give a firm foundation to all the difficult talking? What about protection?

Before she'd reached a conscious decision on what she wanted, her body made the movement. It had a will of its own. She slid her arm over his body and spooned him, feeling his strong back against her stomach and breasts, while her legs tucked themselves in behind his.

He didn't stir.

Again, she lay there, silent and still. She could feel his breathing pushing lightly against her. He'd fallen asleep with his head on her pillow instead of his, and her mouth was only an inch from the neat curve at the back of his head. She liked the fresh haircut, liked the soft, clean feel of the strands brushing against her lips when she eased even closer.

Surely he would wake up now.

But, no.

She moved her hand, sliding it across his stomach and down to his hip and thigh. The muscles there were long and hard, and his skin was so warm and smooth. She let her hand come to rest and listened for a change in his breathing. How long since she'd been this aware of him as they lay side by side in bed?

So long. She couldn't remember.

Before Tyler? Before Abby?

"MJ..." she whispered softly. She was committed to this now. There was no going back.

He moved in his sleep, rolling over onto his stomach. She moved her hand up his body, tracing the line of his backside and then his spine. A wicked and very pleasurable stubbornness set in. He was going to wake up. He just was. She was going to *seduce* him into waking up, and if the seduction took an hour, then so be it.

There was something almost forbidden about it, something very secret, touching a man when he didn't know it, even if the man was her husband. It was easy to forget, in day-to-day life, what a great body he had, what a perfect balance of muscle and bone and width and length and hardness and softness.

Despite how thin it was, the silk of her nightdress felt like too much of a barrier between them. She slipped the straps from her shoulders and peeled the garment down her body until it reached the point where she could kick it to the foot of the bed.

Skin to skin felt so much better. She slid her leg across MJ's body and wrapped her arm around him so that she was half lying on top of him, her breasts squishing into his back and her mound pushing against the rounded muscle of his butt.

MJ, wake up...

He didn't.

She began to kiss him, but she couldn't fully reach his mouth. It was half-buried in the pillow, his head turned to face her and his cheek sunk deep into the beloved sponginess she'd known since childhood. She teased her tongue at the barely accessible corner of his lips, feeling the rub of her breasts on his back as she shifted position to get her mouth closer.

MJ asleep was pretty frustrating as a lover.

Suspiciously frustrating.

He was pretending.

She wasn't sure at what point he had woken up, but somewhere in there—somewhere in among the caresses and half kisses and the playful, frustrated self-pleasuring of her body rubbing against him—he'd realized what was happening and he didn't want her to stop.

She played along.

"MJ, come on, do you want me to make love to you in your dreams?" she whispered and pushed at his shoulder to get him to roll over. He flopped onto his side and then his back, and at last she could press herself right on top of him and ravish that beautiful mouth of his to her heart's content. She could run her hands down his chest; she could feel that deliciously hard, swollen piece of him against her groin and take her time with it.

She must be driving him crazy, and she knew he would have to crack soon. The process of forcing him to crack was delectable. Brushing her hardened nipples across his mouth, straddling him and finding a familiar rhythm, swooping down to plant a trail of kisses along his collarbone and then down, and down, and down.

"You witch," he gasped.

She slid upward, grinning. In the dim room, she could just see his face—eyes finally open, grinning back at her. "Liking this?" she teased softly.

"Every second. Thought it was a dream at first, but then…it was way too good for that. I was afraid it might stop if I really woke up."

"I wasn't planning to stop."

"Good."

"How long have you been pretending?"

"Not measuring the minutes right now. Keep going."

"Close your eyes."

"Can't I keep them open? Just the sight of you. I never get tired of you, Alicia."

Something shafted through her—a charge of sensual delight at the idea he found her this beautiful. She took his face between her palms and kissed him with sweet, lingering heat, taking her mouth away every now and then so that he had to chase her.

He tired of it, tired of the game, and she loved that moment, too. He growled deep in his chest and rolled her onto her back, lavishing his touch all down her body, lavishing his mouth everywhere she wanted until she was moaning with need.

"MJ, please, oh, please." Her breathing was ragged. She reached for him, desperate to guide him into her, but he was already there, sliding slickly into her moist core, filling her until she ached.

She grabbed his shoulders and anchored him in place and he rocked his hips, while her legs tightened around him. She arched and flung her head to the side and all control ripped away from them both, like sails ripping from a mast in a storm, and they rode the storm blissfully until it died away.

Which was when he should have rolled over and fallen asleep, oblivious to her mood.

But he didn't this time. Instead, he pulled her close and held her, and she lay there with her head pillowed on his arm. Once again, they hadn't used protection. She'd thought of it this time, but still he hadn't mentioned it. It occurred to her that maybe the separation in their roles was so great that he simply assumed she was taking care of the matter—that she'd gone back on the Pill without telling him, or that she was confident enough that the timing was safe.

She could actually feel him thinking but not about pregnancy. He'd gone in a different direction, and she could read his mind through the heavy silence. "It was real," she said, before he could ask. "Of course it was real, MJ! Couldn't you tell?"

"I thought I could. But then I wondered. Because it never occurred to me that it wasn't real all those other times." He let out a complicated laugh. "We're such a mess, aren't we? You knew I was thinking about it. Hell!"

"We're not a mess right now." She trailed her fingers down his chest, loving the sense of possession and familiarity. Just loving *him,* because for once they were both living the same moment together, not thinking about something else or existing across a yawning distance from each other.

"Having to discuss whether you faked it or not?" he challenged. "That's not messed up?"

"No, because it's progress." It felt like huge progress, compared to the usual tight feeling she would have had at a moment like this—the feeling that her whole self was shut tight away inside her and that he had no idea.

He thought about the progress idea for a moment, then said, his voice a little scratchy, "I like progress. A lot."

"Me, too."

"This is good. This is so good, Alicia, I can't tell you."

But could they hold on to it?

Chapter Fourteen

The weather forecast proved accurate for Friday. They needed coats and scarves and gloves for their visit to the pumpkin farm, and there weren't many other people there. Still, it was fun.

A ride in a tractor-pulled wagon out to the middle of the pumpkin field, this time, where the ground was littered with enormous orange blobs. Tyler couldn't lift the one he chose, while Abby enjoyed rolling hers along the ground. After they'd loaded the four pumpkins into the car—three for jack-o'-lanterns and one for pie, they decided—there was a hay-filled barn for the children to play in, and it was sheltered and warmer and great fun.

Until the dust from the hay got in their noses and they all began to sneeze.

"Is this our cue to go home?" MJ asked, and he had that look in his eye that Alicia recognized—the restless one that said he was itching to pull out his phone and call the office or the hospital, because living life at a preschooler level was driving him nuts.

This had been nice but not as nice as the apple picking last week. Even with something as simple as this, you couldn't go back; you couldn't repeat your previous success.

What if we're having another baby?

Still, MJ was right; it was their cue to go home. Tyler in particular had red, streaming eyes and a swollen nose, and he was miserable. Any minute and you wouldn't be able to tell where the allergy tears left off and the actual crying tears began. "I hadn't realized he was this allergic to hay," Alicia said. She wondered if Maura had known.

At home, she rinsed off his poor little face, and the sneezing stopped and the redness and swelling began to disappear. At the kitchen table, MJ cut a circular hole in the top of three of the pumpkins and scooped out the filling, and Abby directed him to carve the kinds of faces she wanted—one scary, one loud and one silly.

"How do you make a loud face?" MJ asked.

"You know, Daddy. Like this." She opened her mouth wide and screwed up her face as if she was yelling, and he carved an impressively accurate version of her expression into the pumpkin with his surgeon's expertise, while the sky darkened outside and the predicted rain began to fall.

"Tyler, you make the silly face for me," MJ said, and Tyler watched with total absorption while he reproduced the stretchy grin and lopsided eyes that Tyler had pulled.

"This is the first time I've ever seen you doing surgery," Alicia commented.

"Surgery?" He laughed, and those capable fingers of his paused in their action for a moment. "I guess it is. I hadn't even thought."

"If the orthopedic thing doesn't work out for you, you can always make a living as a pumpkin sculptor."

"Unfortunately the work is seasonal. Otherwise I'd throw away the surgery thing in a heartbeat."

"Mommy and Daddy are being silly," Abby announced.

"Yes, we are," MJ agreed. "We have a new plan now. Mommy and Daddy have to be silly at least twice every week and six times on Tuesdays." He threw Alicia a quick look, and she nodded and laughed back at him.

"That is *so* silly!" Abby said.

"Anybody want hot chocolate and cheese on toast for lunch?" Alicia asked.

Everyone said yes, and MJ finished carving the last pumpkin just before Alicia had the meal ready. They sat at the kitchen table to eat, admiring the pumpkins now sitting on the countertop, with the sweet, earthy smell of the pulp and seeds still in the air.

When Tyler went down for his nap after lunch and Abby was sitting with her pencils and a sketchpad at the coffee table in the front room, busily drawing, MJ asked Alicia in the kitchen, "So? Good day so far?"

"Very. They've had fun. Have you?"

"I was ready to jump ship when Tyler's sneezing got so bad, but he pulled out of that pretty well." He hung a dish towel on the handle of the oven door, and she registered that during the time she'd been upstairs with Tyler, he'd cleared away the lunchtime mess, loaded the dishwasher, wiped down the countertops.

"We left at the right time," she agreed. "I had the impression you were a little bored."

"Well…yeah." He looked regretful. "Do you think the kids picked up on it?"

"No, you pretended well."

"So I fake things, too, sometimes, don't I?"

"I guess faking pleasure can be an act of kindness and love."

He put his arms around her. "Or an act of anger."

"That, too." She hugged him back, feeling closer to him over the past twenty-four hours and closer to seeing a future with him than she'd felt in months. "Thank you for clearing up."

"No problem. It's not like I have to do it a lot. Maybe we could have an agreement," he suggested, going back to the real topic. "That we only ever fake what we feel if it's for the right reasons."

She laughed. "Who determines those? Do we need a contract?"

"We have a contract," he reminded her, still with his arms around her. "Marriage is a contract."

"We're negotiating some amendments."

"That's okay."

"MJ, I...really appreciate—" But she didn't know how to finish.

He did it for her. "How hard I'm trying?"

"Yes."

"Could we see if Andy and Claudia would be willing to babysit tonight?" he suggested, pulling away. She could see he was energized by the idea and that this little peaceful interlude was over. He needed something to be happening. The only time he ever tolerated downtime was when he was exhausted from work. "We could go out for dinner. I liked the place we went when they announced their engagement. They'll remember the name of it. I'll talk to Claudia and call the restaurant right now, see if I can make a reservation."

She was supposed to tell him it was a wonderful idea. Problem was, dressing up to go to an upmarket French restaurant wasn't what she felt like at all. Six months ago—

even three weeks ago—she wouldn't have said a word, would have nodded and smiled and said yes, with an impeccable performance of enthusiasm, and then spent an hour and a half getting dressed. Pleasing MJ and agreeing with exactly what he wanted was her role, her side of the bargain.

She almost did it today, too, but if he was trying hard, rethinking so much, then she needed to match his effort. She took a steadying breath. "I love half of that plan."

"Which half?" He looked down at her, loosening his hold a little.

"The half where Andy and Claudia babysit and we go out."

"That's pretty much the whole plan, isn't it?"

"Okay, so I love seventy-five percent of it. But could we change the venue? Just go to a bar and have burgers or steaks? With fries? And soda or beer? And a jukebox or big-screen TV, or something?"

She felt the muscles of his forearms tense against her back. "I wanted to make it something special, a celebration."

"It can still be special, at a bar. The special part of it is the two of us, not the venue, or what we eat, or how we look to other people. I just don't want to dress up, that's all. I don't want to feel like I'm on show. I want us just to be two people having a relaxed night out."

"As opposed to what? I'm not getting this, Alicia." She could feel how impatient he was as he pulled out of their embrace. He wanted to stride along the front porch to Andy's front door right now and get this whole big, beautiful plan kicked into high gear.

"As opposed to successful Manhattan surgeon Dr. Michael McKinley Junior and his beautiful wife dine at this year's hot new five-star restaurant. As opposed to the kind of thing that looks as if we're waiting for the camera flash and an appearance in next week's social pages."

"I thought you wanted that. You always look so fabulous when we're at a charity event. You spend so much time on it."

"Because you like for me to look good. And it's not like I want to dress like a gargoyle..."

"Yeah, their fashion sense is—"

No, don't joke right now, MJ.

"But it puts me under pressure," she interrupted. "It makes it harder for me to be myself. There are times when I feel like dressing down a little. And I think I really need to be myself if—if what we're trying to do has a chance of success."

"You fake it that much?" he asked quietly. "You don't just fake orgasm—you fake our whole marriage."

"No!"

"It's pretty much what you just said."

"I—I don't— I fake some of it, some of the public part."

"You say yes to things you don't remotely want. You act the role that you think I'm asking for, even when it's not the real you at all. You pretend you're happy when you're actually miserable."

"Only sometimes."

He was silent. She'd really shocked him. She hadn't thought it was that dark a confession, but apparently it was.

"Why?" he finally asked.

"To please you."

"Why?"

"Because that's what you want from the partnership."

Another shocked silence, then he said, "Not to that extent. Not if it's not working."

"It isn't working," she said, trying to be gentle about it.

But how could she? It came out blunt, and she just couldn't help it. "Isn't that already clear?"

"We'll go to a bar, then. Wear whatever you like. Let me talk to Claudia and see if it's even possible. I'll call Andy on his cell, if she and Ben aren't at home." He did what he'd been itching to do and went next door, where Claudia was still working on unpacking her things from the city whenever Ben was napping or contentedly awake.

Alicia waited, admiring Abby's drawings, and then heard MJ's impatient male footsteps coming back along the porch.

"She says they'd love to," he reported. "I told her six o'clock. Is that all right?"

"Yes, perfect. That way, we'll be back in time to step in if they're having trouble getting Tyler to settle."

But MJ was the one having trouble settling, for the rest of the afternoon. He wasn't used to this kind of a schedule. His need for downtime was very low. He went for a run, played on the floor with Abby for a quarter of an hour, looking at his watch every five minutes.

Alicia felt like his jailer and finally told him, "If you need to call the office or the hospital, why don't you do that? It's Friday afternoon. If anything has come up, I'm thinking you don't want to leave it too late in the day."

He probably wasn't aware of how relieved he looked. "Would you mind? There are a couple of patients—"

"Call. Sit in the bedroom, so it's quiet if Tyler wakes up or Abby gets noisy."

He spent forty minutes on the phone and emerged from the bedroom looking much happier, as if he'd put the whole medical world right again. Alicia felt a complicated rush of love. He was such a doctor! She was proud of him for that. But this afternoon's talk still hung over them, as did the question in the back of her mind about the other night and the possibility of a baby, and she knew they'd only shelved things, not solved them.

Dinner.

Dinner would be good, just the two of them.

Alicia hadn't wanted to dress up, but she looked incredible anyhow. She came down the stairs in snug-fitting jeans and a stretchy, beaded black top that hugged her figure and showed off the perfect shape of her lightly tanned collarbone.

"Ready to go next door, kids? We'll take some toys with us, okay? Help me pack the dinosaurs into the tub."

All four of them got down on the carpet and threw the plastic creatures into the container, with Alicia directing Tyler, who was more inclined to keep playing than to pack away. She had twisted and pinned up her hair in a couple of casual coils, and when she leaned across the carpet to pick up another dinosaur, MJ saw that she was wearing the diamond hair clip he'd given her in Las Vegas seven years ago—the gift that should have been a ring.

It seemed significant that she was wearing it, but MJ didn't know if it was.

His emotions were all over the place today—hope and shock and boredom and need—and he couldn't keep living like this.

They'd slept together twice since their supposed separation, and yet sex hadn't sealed anything or solved anything. He hadn't used protection and she hadn't said a word. He wanted to ask her about it but didn't want to risk making an issue out of something that might not be an issue at all, when they had so much else to resolve.

They had to get something worked out. He understood why Alicia didn't want to be rushed into a decision, but... dammit! He was heading back to Manhattan tomorrow and very much doubted he'd be able to get up here again until he came for Andy and Claudia's wedding next weekend. Were they going to fake their way through that, too?

It took a good ten minutes or more to get the kids organized at Andy and Claudia's, and for once MJ appreciated his brother's laid-back attitude. "Listen, I have a key to the apartment," Andy said, "so if you've forgotten something, it's no big deal, and we can take them back next door for bedtime if you're not back. We have a spare baby monitor. We can set that up. We actually can handle this."

"I'm sorry," Alicia apologized. "Tyler's going through a tricky stage with his sleep patterns. I don't want to put you through a horrible evening."

"You won't."

"Well, okay..."

She wasn't normally so protective or anxious about the children and neither was MJ. He thought that in both of them it was a symptom of their uncertainty, the rocking of the whole foundation of their lives. He was very glad when they were finally in the car, heading for the bar Andy had recommended, where there would be a wood fire burning in a big stone fireplace and a dark corner where they would have quiet and privacy.

The place was as warm and pleasant as Andy had promised, with the TV tuned to a sports channel in the opposite corner so that it didn't dominate, just provided some background movement and sound. They ordered soups and steaks. Alicia didn't want wine or beer but had soda instead, so MJ simply ordered a glass of red to complement his steak, and it went down in easy sips over the course of the meal.

The food was good. They talked about it. Hearty soup. Tender steak. Tangy salad. All very polite.

Alicia presented him with the problem of Tyler's nap,

and he voted for having him give it up. A big sleep and then a late bedtime wasn't such a problem in the summer, when it stayed light until nine and you could go to the park in the evening. Coming into winter as they now were, it might be easier to push him through the afternoon, if it meant he would then go down at night by seven.

When this was settled, there was nothing more to hide behind.

"I want to talk about the partnership," MJ said. "If there's anything more we need to put on the table, then let's put it there. Right now." He knew he sounded too impatient, too formal and too angry, but this was killing him.

Killing them both.

Or was he making too many assumptions, yet again? Thinking he knew her, thinking her feelings reflected his, when they didn't at all? When she was only faking it to please him.

She was looking at him helplessly, and that was exactly how he felt, too.

Helpless.

Alicia, why did you marry me?

"You're wearing the hair clip," he said.

"I love it." She touched her hair and smiled, and his groin tightened the way it so often did. "I've always loved it."

"You didn't when I first gave it to you. You were visibly disappointed that it wasn't a ring."

"MJ—"

But he was nowhere near done. "You were waiting for me to ask you, and then you thought I wasn't going to, and there was this look of disappointment on your face that I couldn't stand, and I just wanted to fix it. It all seemed so clear and perfect that night."

"It was, in so many ways. Since then—"

Still he ignored her, because he didn't believe her. She was just echoing what she thought he wanted, the way she always did. "I thought we got married for the best reasons in the world," he said. "Not everyone else's reasons, not this starry-eyed idea of true love and effortless happiness. Our reasons were better. They would last because they were real, I thought. They were grounded. They weren't naive."

"No. They were never that." What was that in her voice? Wistfulness? He couldn't pursue that right now.

"But now you tell me you've faked so much of what I thought made us happy, Alicia. The sense of partnership, the satisfaction with our different roles. Tell me the truth about why you married me."

"The truth?"

"It was the money. The security. Wasn't it?"

"I was desperate. I didn't give myself—"

"So that's a yes?"

Again, she tried to soften it, skirt around the edge of the truth with excuses and explanations. "MJ, it wasn't as—"

But he wasn't going to let the excuses happen tonight. He didn't want to hear them. He wanted it straight. Needed it straight.

"So that's a yes," he repeated forcefully. "Say it, Alicia!"

She lifted her chin. Her eyes had narrowed in distress, and he thought there might have been tears glinting there, behind the screen of lashes. "Yes."

He swore, but it came out more like the grunt from a body blow than an actual word. "I always thought…" He didn't recognize his own voice. Picked up and tried again. "I always knew…that there was an element of that. Of course I did. I knew your situation. Filled in the blanks.

But I thought I had more to offer. I thought everything would deepen."

"You did. It did. I—"

He barely heard. More excuses and skirting around. More faking. He wasn't interested. "Funny how you can believe something in your secret heart, but it's never really true, at some level, until you say it or hear it said out loud."

MJ was right. It was weird and horrible—what a difference it made to actually admit to the truth in words.

They sat across the dimly lit table from each other. Another group of diners laughed loudly at someone's joke. A waitress skimmed past and skillfully and cheerfully handed out beers at the next table. The door opened and a couple came in. The world went on just as usual, as her marriage to MJ did its final slow-motion collapse into the dust.

He didn't want her excuses or her rationale, she thought. He just wanted it straight, and now he had it. She'd married him for the money and security, and this devil's bargain right at the start had haunted them both for seven years. He was right to think that the poison from it had seeped through to the present, and it was clear he wasn't about to let it seep into the future, as well.

This time, he was the one to make the decision that their marriage was over.

He stood up and made a mimed scribble in the air— the universal sign for wanting the check. "I'll take you home," he said.

"MJ, we can talk about this more. We've been doing so well with—"

"There's nothing to say. I could forgive the reason. I could understand and forgive how you felt back then, but what you've said the past week or so about faking ever since. Faking so damned much!" He shook his head. "That's the kicker. That's the killer. That nothing ever changed. That you married me for those reasons and you've still been faking, after seven years."

He was reeling. She felt as if she'd delivered him a death blow, and there was nothing she could think of to say that would make this any better, because he wouldn't believe it now.

"Leaving me. Leaving that note. Was that just an attempt to get more leverage?"

"No!"

"Worked pretty well. I've been bending over backward."

"I know you have. I've—"

"Well done!" he cut in. "Impressive strategy."

She was right in what she'd thought. He wouldn't believe anything. No point in protesting the word *strategy*. No point in doing anything but bowing her head and accepting the blow.

"I'll take you back to Andy's, then I'll head down to the city," MJ said with a crisp, new decisiveness in his tone.

She knew he was hurting, but he was hiding it with the same drive and discipline he gave to his long hours of surgery, and there was nothing she could do about the hurting because his trust was gone, and she understood why.

"I'll be back up Friday night for the wedding," he said. "We won't say anything to anyone about the divorce until after that. It's not fair to the family. I won't spoil Andy and Claudia's day." A long breath hissed in between his clenched teeth. "If this marriage has been faked for seven years, it can be faked for a little longer."

Chapter Fifteen

The days dragged unbearably after MJ had left.

He'd packed up his things as soon as they arrived home from the bar and was gone within fifteen minutes. When Abby and Tyler flung themselves into the big bed the next morning and found Daddy not there, it took every bit of Alicia's willpower to put a bright face on his absence.

"Daddy had work to do at the hospital and couldn't stay. He's coming again on Friday, because Uncle Andy and Aunt Claudia are getting married. He was sad to go, but we can talk to him on the phone."

Faking it.

Again.

"*Aunt* Claudia?"

"Yes, she's going to be your aunt now, and Ben is your cousin."

"Friday is miles away," Abby observed sadly. "How many sleeps?"

"Six."

"That is too many."

"I know. But we'll keep busy, and Friday will come."

They kept busy.

Playgrounds and stories and DVDs. Blocks and puzzles and library and shopping. Baths and hide-and-seek and running through piles of leaves.

And cooking.

The only time Alicia ever felt close to holding it together was when she was cooking. She made pumpkin pie and Halloween cookies, pizza and pumpkin chili, meat loaf and chocolate-pumpkin muffins and another apple cake to freeze, using up the last of their pickings. She was good at this, she realized. Not just the cooking itself but the organizing. Even with Abby's and Tyler's "help" the process and the results were good.

Could this possibly be a window into something positive about the future? She could take some classes in catering and baking and commercial kitchen management, find the right location and open her own business. It would be a long-range project, not something she would accomplish overnight, but as an idea, it had a lot of promise. A tiny flicker of optimism came into her heart, like a candle flame in a darkened room. At least she might have something that was truly her own.

Claudia smelled all the baking smells, received a generous share of the muffins and cookies and said on Tuesday, when she'd brought Ben next door for an afternoon play with his big cousins, "I've been wondering, Alicia... The restaurant said they'd do a cake for us if we wanted, but it's not really their area. They'd rather have one brought in. Would you be interested?"

"You want me to make your wedding cake?" Alicia

wasn't even sure she'd understood correctly. "You'd trust me with something like that?"

"I love the way you bake. Of course I'd trust you. It's not like it's a wedding for three hundred people."

Alicia felt the pricking of the tears that had been so close to the surface for days. Claudia had started to become a friend, probably the only person in the McKinley clan who didn't suspect the truth about MJ and Alicia's flawed marital bargain. And now she'd articulated something that meshed right in with Alicia's own thinking about her future. Still, life had taught Alicia to be cautious about a few things.

"A wedding cake is a lot different to little treats for the kids," she said to her soon-to-be sister-in-law.

"If you don't want to…"

"Oh, it's not that. Really, it isn't. I'm just afraid I'd let you down, that's all. That the cake wouldn't turn out the way you wanted."

"We can work together, pick a recipe and style that you're confident about. If you want to. I'm stressing that, Alicia. Only if you want to."

"I'd love to, if you really do trust me."

"Of course I trust you!" She leaned across the couch and gave Alicia a hug, and it was almost too much.

So after Ben and Abby and Tyler were asleep that night, Alicia and Claudia spent the evening on the internet and chose recipes for cake, filling and frosting, as well as colors and decorating styles. On Wednesday Alicia shopped for ingredients and equipment, on Thursday she baked, and on Friday she filled and decorated.

The cake was as pretty and stylish as a wedding dress, with two round layers of smooth frosting, piped pink ribbons and roses, and flavors of vanilla and strawberry within. Andy and Claudia were thrilled with the result, and the whole process, with its beckoning suggestion of a future career, was the only bearable thing about the whole week.

By Friday night, the finished cake sat in the refrigerator, carefully covered.

Friday night, when the rest of the McKinley family came up from the city, MJ included.

His parents arrived first—the intimidating pair in whose company Alicia still didn't feel at ease, even after seven years. She called them Michael and Helen, and Helen called her "Alicia dear" and approved of the way she was raising the children and the way she helped organize family functions, but Alicia felt there was a degree of reserve in the older woman, all the same. Her father-in-law, Michael, always greeted her with a hug and a few words and then left her alone. He didn't seem to know what to say to her, and whether he approved of her as a daughter-in-law was hard to know.

For her part, the Michael-and-Helen bit didn't come easily to Alicia. She always felt it should be Doctor and Mrs. McKinley, but that would be weird, to address her own parents-in-law so formally.

They had brought MJ's aunt Carol, Helen's sister and her husband, Gary, while Claudia's dad and stepmother arrived about forty minutes later from Pennsylvania. Her mom and stepfather would be coming up from New York City tomorrow morning, as would her best friend, Kelly, and her husband.

These were pretty much the only guests. MJ had two uncles on the McKinley side, each with medical connections and adult children of their own, but all those McKinleys were busy and scattered all over the country, and they hadn't been invited. Andy and Claudia weren't kidding when they said they wanted their wedding small.

There were only going to be around twenty-five people at tomorrow's ceremony and dinner, while tonight they'd decided against a formal pre-wedding meal and gone for a very casual feast of take-out Chinese at home. It was an unusual way to prepare for a wedding, but there was a warmth and intimacy to it that Alicia would have liked, if she hadn't been so tense.

Staying well away from center stage as she always did at family gatherings, she caught all the looks Andy and Claudia gave each other—secret and hot, or sharing a private joke, or making a wordless promise. Scarlett and Daniel were the same. Sometimes they didn't even need to look at each other. They would reach out and touch, or move like dancers echoing each other's pose.

That was what love really meant. That was what Alicia wanted, but it wasn't going to happen.

At eight-thirty in the evening, MJ was the only one expected but not yet here. "Do you know when we should expect him, Alicia dear?" Helen asked.

"Pretty soon. He texted from the hospital at three, saying he hoped to get away within the next hour."

"So I should double that to two hours, to be on the safe side?"

"I think he would have texted again if he was going to be that much later than he said."

Would he, though? He'd been so good about it last week, updating her with an almost to-the-minute prediction about his arrival time, but the situation was very different now.

They'd spoken on the phone three times but only so that she could then put Abby and Tyler on for a chat with Daddy. Abby was happy to give lengthy detail about her day, but Tyler didn't really understand the phone and just listened in silence with a smile on his face while MJ did all the work, then pretty soon held out the phone again for Alicia to take. "It's me again, MJ."

"Okay, he's still too little for this."

"He loves hearing your voice, though."

Those moments had been very stiff and hadn't lasted long. The distance between them, filled with emotion, was palpable to each other and so hard to hide from the kids.

"Do you think he'll want to eat?" Helen asked now.

"I expect so. He won't have stopped on the way. Sometimes he says he's eaten and it turns out to be one banana or a stale muffin."

"Was there enough left?"

"There was plenty," Alicia assured her. "I didn't want to leave it out until he got here." The remnants of the meal had been put away, and everyone was lingering over coffee and tea in Andy and Claudia's living room, after the children had been put to bed. Alicia had a baby monitor close by, so she could hear and quickly respond if Abby or Tyler woke up next door, but there had been no sounds so far.

"This is him," Scarlett said, as lights shone in the driveway.

Alicia's heart thumped heavily and she felt ill. The evening had been so relaxed until now. The noise of family conversation had disguised her underlying tension, and with the two new members of the McKinley clan—Andy's Claudia, and Scarlett's Daniel—still getting to know everyone, while Claudia's dad and stepmother were new faces in the circle, also, she hadn't felt that she was the only one who didn't belong.

But now MJ was here.

She stood up instinctively, and everyone went quiet, looking at her. Oh, it was her face! She'd forgotten to put on her mask. Quickly she rectified the situation, schooling her features into a relaxed smile as she moved toward the door.

His footsteps sounded slower than usual, coming onto the porch. He felt the same dread as she did, but this wasn't enough to link them together tonight.

She opened the door for him, since this was what everyone else seemed to expect. They were hanging back. Or, no, Helen had already gone to the kitchen to get the takeout boxes out of the refrigerator so that MJ could choose what he wanted and reheat it in the microwave.

"Hi," he said.

"Hi… Did you have a good drive up?"

"It was fine. No real slow points once I got onto the thruway." He leaned forward and kissed her cheek without touching her.

Without even looking at her, really.

He wasn't as good at faking it as she was. The way his eyes skated away and his body stiffened told her clearly that the distance between them hadn't lessened during the week. She dreaded the possibility of someone in the family picking up on it.

But then, as if he'd suddenly thought about this, too, he pulled her into his arms and said, "I've missed you. How're the kids?"

"Good. Asleep."

"That's good," he answered mechanically. "How has Tyler been managing without his nap?"

"Falling into his food by dinnertime, then out like a light. I think it was the right thing."

"Good. That's good."

Helen appeared. "MJ, Alicia says you won't have eaten."

"No, I haven't."

"Come and heat something up. There's plenty." She headed back toward the kitchen, speaking over her shoulder. "I know you like General Tso's chicken…." Unknowingly, Helen was taking the pressure off both of them.

But it didn't last. "Alicia has made us the most gorgeous wedding cake, MJ," Claudia said. "I had no idea she could bake so well."

"Neither did I, until this past week," MJ answered tightly. "She's been full of surprises lately."

Alicia caught Andy's narrow-eyed glance. He was the only one who would be able to decode the layers. She wished with all her heart that she hadn't told him about the prospect of divorce, but at the time she hadn't been able to hold the words back.

"I'm itching to show it off to you, on her behalf," Claudia was saying, oblivious. "But it's next door, in your refrigerator. Alicia, you will show him later, won't you?"

"Isn't it like the wedding gown?" MJ joked. "Shouldn't it be a secret from everyone until it's unveiled on the day?"

He and Alicia hadn't had a wedding cake at all.

If I'd waited and said I wanted a proper wedding, with family, would all this be happening now?

But it was a pointless question. She hadn't had the courage to wait back then, even though this wasn't the first time she wished that she had. She'd been so afraid MJ would change his mind. She'd been like a greedy child who couldn't take her eyes off the candy in case someone snatched it away. She would have married him right there at the Las Vegas restaurant table, if there'd been a priest standing by. And there would have been no family on her side for her to invite, even if they'd waited a year to be married.

"I'll show you the wedding gown, too, if you like," Claudia said.

But Helen came back from the kitchen again and uttered a cry of protest. "I won't let you disregard tradition to that extent, Claudia," she said. "It is *incredibly* bad luck if the groom has seen the gown before the ceremony, and I want your marriage to last!"

MJ and Alicia said nothing. She wondered if his thoughts had gone in the same direction as hers. Her dress hadn't been a wedding gown at all, just a cocktail dress with a dubious pedigree from a vintage clothing store. And of course MJ had seen it before.

As for the bad luck, it was much more than bad luck at the root of the failure of their marriage.

"Can I heat up something to eat now, Mom?" he said.

"I've already put it in the microwave, a little bit of everything and fried rice. You can go back for seconds. There's still plenty. We over-ordered."

"You have to over-order when it's a family get-together like this," Aunt Carol said.

Everyone had their own very firm ideas about how to celebrate around the edges of a wedding. MJ ate, more coffee and tea was served, and the family conversation continued until almost eleven before Andy called a halt, after a whispered exchange with Helen.

"My bride needs her beauty sleep, according to Mom. Me, I think she'd look reasonably okay on no sleep at all for a week, but I'm bowing to the expert opinion."

Claudia slapped him on the arm, but his announcement had broken up the gathering.

"It's hard to imagine there's going to be a wedding tomorrow," Helen said rather wistfully, to herself more than anyone else. Alicia didn't know if anyone else had heard. She realized that the older woman was more disappointed than she was letting on about the fact that none of her children seemed destined to have the large, elaborate New York City wedding she would have enjoyed.

Scarlett and Daniel went back to his place, Claudia's

dad and stepmother retired to Andy's spare room, Aunt Carol and Uncle Gary went off to their bed-and-breakfast inn, and Helen and Michael accompanied MJ and Alicia next door, because they were sleeping here, in the main bedroom, while MJ and Alicia were using the sofa bed in the living room downstairs.

Crunch time for both of them, in the faking-it department.

"I feel so bad that you're giving up your bed for us," Helen said. She picked up one of the fresh, folded towels Alicia had laid on the comforter.

"Oh, Helen, you don't," Michael scoffed. The two of them were often impatient with each other like this. "We could have gone to a bed-and-breakfast place, like Carol and Gary, if you'd felt bad. You wanted to be here, in the center of the action, and you love having a daughter-in-law who does the right thing about giving up her bed."

"Well, I do love that," Helen agreed, "which is why I like to tell her that I appreciate her."

"So tell her you appreciate her, not that you feel bad." Michael snatched up the second towel from the bed, in readiness for heading to the bathroom.

He seemed tired and irritable tonight, red in the face and a little steamy. He was well into his sixties now and still trying to work like a man of half that age. Helen could never persuade him to slow down. A month or two ago she had wrung from him the promise that he would retire three years from now, and he seemed to feel that this deadline required him to work even harder until it came.

Helen gave an exasperated sigh at his words. "I think she knows what I really mean."

She reached out and gave Alicia an awkward hug, as Michael stomped past her and out the open bedroom door. Alicia was glad that MJ was downstairs and not a witness to the hug, because he probably wouldn't have trusted the way she squeezed Helen back. Did she deserve this much support from her mother-in-law? Right now, she simply appreciated the older woman, with a rush of affection she didn't fully want to show.

Sometimes the real feelings could be harder than the fake ones. She was so fragile about any kind of emotion right now.

Hormonal and fragile?

She would know any day. Monday. If her period hadn't come by Monday, she would take a test.

A baby. How disastrous would that be? She couldn't even imagine.

But the imaginings played out like reels of film all the same, as she lay sleeplessly in the sofa bed beside MJ a little later.

They'd barely spoken making their preparations for bed. She had climbed in first. He'd told her, "I'll get the light," and he'd turned it off and then gone into the kitchen for a glass of water, while she lay there for a few minutes, waiting for the moment when his weight would change the feel of the thin fold-down mattress and stretchy springs.

Now, more than an hour later, he seemed to be asleep, although she thought he had lain awake for quite a while, also. For her, sleep was still miles away.

Was she pregnant?

Too early for any symptoms to show in her body. She thought about the ones she remembered from Abby and Tyler—the sore breasts, the heightened sensitivity to tastes and smells. Those hadn't kicked in this soon, she was sure.

How would she tell MJ if she was having his baby? How would he react? Would anything change?

She remembered last week, the way she'd lain beside him wakefully while he was already asleep. This was so different. No question tonight of reaching out to caress him, wakening him gradually with the touch of her body and her mouth.

He began to dream. She heard the change in his breathing and then a groan and some unintelligible words escaping his lips. It wasn't a happy dream. Wasn't that ironic and sad and strange? They were both so unhappy and powerless to make anything better.

She stretched her hand toward him, found the loose hem of his silk pajama top and held on to it for comfort, the way she still sometimes held on to her pillow. If she didn't grip too tightly, and if she didn't pull the slippery fabric closer, he wouldn't know. Her hand burrowed a little closer to his body. Close enough to feel the warmth. Almost close enough to touch.

She felt sleep creeping up on her at last.

Chapter Sixteen

The weather smiled on Claudia and Andy for their wedding day, and everything went without a hitch, from her trip to the hairdresser in the morning, to the simple church ceremony in the late afternoon.

The air was cold and crisp but the sun shone brightly and there was no wind. The fall color was only just past its peak, and the white church they'd chosen, with its high, pointed steeple, was so typical of Vermont that it could have been photographed for a magazine, especially with the gorgeous bride and smiling groom standing on its front steps.

They looked so happy—relieved that the solemn part was safely over, exultant in the prospect of their future together. Claudia wore an ankle-length, figure-hugging gown in the softest blush pink, with close-fitting sleeves in sheer, shimmery lace. Against her dark hair and beautiful skin, the color and style were magical. Andy could barely take his eyes off her long enough to face the camera and smile.

The bride and groom weren't the only ones who needed to smile for the photographer. Travis wasn't a full-time professional but a serious part-timer, the brother of Andy's friend Chris, who had volunteered his services in order to enhance his portfolio. Andy and Claudia wanted the full gamut of bridal couple, bridal party, parents and siblings, and whole family groupings, and Travis was only too happy to have a wide range of shots of such a good-looking and visibly happy pair.

There was a little awkwardness with Claudia's parents, as her mother and father had both remarried and weren't on especially good terms with each other, but it was nothing compared to the awkwardness Alicia felt when she and MJ stood in a formal pose with Abby and Tyler, against the backdrop of white church and brilliant leaves.

"The two of you together," coached Chris's brother, "and the kids in front. Alicia, if you could put your hand on Abby's shoulder? MJ, arm around your wife?" Both of them did as Travis had asked, but MJ's arm was stiff and unyielding and pulled at the shoulder of her silk dress. The photographer added after a moment, "Tyler, buddy, can you stand still and give us a smile?"

The light was beginning to fade by this point. Having changed the venue for their ceremony at such short notice, Andy and Claudia had had to fit in at four-thirty after another couple, whose wedding had been at two. There were still drifts of confetti on the ground from the previous event, and Tyler kept wanting to get down on his hands and knees to pick up the enticing, colorful handfuls.

"Tyler, please stand up like you've been told," MJ said, losing patience with him. "I can't take much more of this," he muttered under his breath, and Alicia didn't know if it was Tyler pushing his buttons, or the fact that she and MJ were standing together, touching each other and trying to smile, pretending to be happy together, with the folds of her dress brushing his leg, when in reality their emotional distance was so great.

"Maybe if you pick him up," Alicia suggested.

Without a word, MJ leaned down and swung Tyler up in his arms, and he came between them, his body wriggling at first and then settling as MJ said sternly, "If you hold still for a minute, we'll be done."

Alicia caught the scent of balsam and sandalwood from MJ's grooming products, while the fine, expensive weave of his suit sleeve brushed her arm as he took a tiny step away. He was using Tyler's presence in his arms to create physical distance between them, and she wondered if his feelings would turn bitter enough that he would eventually use his children that way emotionally, too.

Surely he wouldn't.

And yet the anger ran deep. She recognized it because it was such a familiar feeling. Where was her own anger now?

Swamped by the far greater strength in her sense of loss. She missed him so much, even now when he was standing right beside her. She'd been wrong to be so angry these past few years, when she was so much to blame herself. She should have had the courage to reach out and ask for more. She should have had more faith that MJ would be willing to give it to her.

If they could just start again, start from the beginning. *If I'm pregnant...*

She wanted it, suddenly, with a force and certainty that almost made her gasp. It didn't make sense. She knew that couples sometimes tried to cement their crumbling marriage with a baby and it rarely—if ever—worked, and yet she wanted it anyway. There was no logic to it, just emotion, and there was no point trying to understand it or pep talk it away.

"Smile, you guys," Travis said. "This is a wedding, not a funeral."

"Sorry," MJ apologized quickly. "My struggling son is not helping."

"I'm cold," Abby complained.

Alicia plastered on her bright model smile, the one she'd bestowed on MJ that very first day in the restaurant almost seven years ago, but today he didn't even see it, the way he hadn't seemed to notice her outfit, with its softly flattering cut and cool-toned fabric. He was too busy staring resolutely into the camera, wearing a teeth-baring grin that didn't reach his eyes.

"That was great," said their photographer-slash-torturer. "We're losing the light. Andy, Claudia, anything else you wanted? Maybe the bridal party over against the trees while they're still catching the last of the sun?"

Andy and Claudia were enthusiastic about this plan, which let Alicia and MJ off the hook. "It's after five-thirty," he muttered. "What time are we due at the restaurant?"

"Not until six-thirty, for cocktail hour."

"Cocktail hour? What time are we sitting down to eat?"

"Seven. Cocktail half hour, I should say."

"Can we arrive at seven, skip the cocktails? Otherwise it'll be a long evening with the kids. Are they going to hold up for the whole time? Should we take a couple of books and toys? We need a sitter. Or better, another nanny. Please hire someone, Alicia." Through all of this he didn't meet her eye, and they didn't touch.

"On your dime?" she asked.

"Of course on my dime! They're still my kids, even

though we're—" He stopped, realizing that he'd let his voice rise too much. Someone would hear, and they weren't done with faking, yet.

If I'm pregnant...

She would have to hire someone. Managing another baby on her own, with no family support, especially if she was trying to study with a view to starting her own business, would be incredibly hard. MJ wouldn't want it. He would be concerned about the effect an exhausted and overcommitted mother would have on his children's well-being, when they were still so young.

She wished she wasn't so financially dependent on him, but there was no choice. Even if she did make some proud gesture about doing without his support, he wouldn't allow it. And she wouldn't make such a gesture. They both had the same reason.

For the children.

"I guess if we have to leave early, that's not such a problem," MJ said much more quietly.

"Because then the performance comes to an end?"

"Yes." He looked at her at last, his eyes swimming with anger and pain, and she couldn't stand how this was hurting them both. He looked tired and strained, and she ached to reach out and touch his face, soothe the tension out of it with a cool, soft hand.

"I love you, MJ," she said, her voice cracking.

He gave a harsh laugh that told her he didn't believe her. "Bit late for that."

"That's rich, coming from you." The words gushed out, tripping over each other. "You've never said it to me. Ever. In seven years. Not until last week, and how could I believe it then?"

His eyes widened in shock. "I showed it in a thousand ways."

Helen came up to them, with little Ben in her arms. "Carol and Gary have suggested we come back to their inn for coffee until it's time to go to the restaurant," she said. "Andy and Claudia are having some more photos taken back at the house with Ben and meeting us there." She frowned, seeing too late that she'd interrupted something, and added quickly, "Anyway, only if you want. Maybe you're going back to Andy's, too."

"I don't know what we're doing," MJ said.

Abby was shivering. Her frilly, high-waisted dress had no warmth to it. "I don't mind, as long as we get the kids inside," Alicia said.

"Tell me what you want and what's best," MJ commanded, and she realized how much he deferred to her when it came to the children's needs and schedule. He trusted this side of their partnership, even now, but she didn't know if he understood that himself.

"Back to Andy's," she decided.

"There'll be no chance to talk," he warned.

"Maybe a bit. Now, even."

"Okay, then I stand by what I just said. A thousand ways, Alicia," he repeated.

They walked to the car, with Abby and Tyler running ahead, both MJ and Alicia knowing that Helen was still watching them, curious and concerned.

"So you're saying you did love me," Alicia said in a low voice, keeping a constant eye out to check that no one could possibly overhear.

"Of course I'm saying that." He spoke with the same quiet carefulness. They were carrying a bomb together, and if they raised their voices it would go off. She was so aware of him walking beside her. To continue talking like this without being heard he had to stay closer to her than either of them wanted.

"From the beginning?" she asked.

"If you trust the word."

"The word *beginning?*"

"The word *love,* of course. No, you're right, I wouldn't have used it back then. But don't make that into a problem. Doesn't mean the love wasn't there."

"Why shouldn't I make it into a problem? It is one, isn't it? For both of us. *In* both of us. That we didn't start out the right way."

They reached the car. Abby and Tyler were standing beside it, waiting for the doors to be unlocked. MJ pressed the button and the car whooped at them. He and Alicia each opened one of the rear doors. Abby could fasten herself into her car seat, but Tyler needed help with the straps and buckle. Alicia bent over him, fumbling before the right clicking sound happened.

"People use the *L* word all the time and it means nothing," MJ said as he climbed into the driver's seat. "They spray it around like air freshener and for the same reason. *I love you. I love you so much.* To pretend that everything is sweet, when it's not. I would rather show it than say it, any day." He started the engine. Carol and Gary were just ahead of them, slowing to check for traffic before turning out of the lot and into the street.

"What you showed…was as much about all sorts of other things as it was about love," Alicia said.

"What things?"

"Pride of possession, keeping your side of the bargain, being the ideal couple."

He rammed the palm of his hand on the steering wheel. "That's what you think? That's all you think it was? Hell, did you even try to understand me?"

"I tried all the time. I'm still trying."

"You tried to *read* me. That's different. I didn't see it then, but I can now."

"Maybe I did try to read you. Because I was scared."

"Scared?"

"That you'd be sorry we'd done it. That I wouldn't match up. I felt I needed to try my utmost, all the time."

"Faking it."

"You think my reasons for that are terrible, but they're not. I had so many good reasons for faking things. I didn't want to. It just happened. I slid into it."

MJ said nothing to this. The two little beings in the back of the car were very silent, also. Tyler surely couldn't understand any of this, but Abby always kept her ears pricked so suspiciously when adults were talking. Alicia didn't want her questions, didn't want to have to lie to her.

"Let's stop for now," she added.

"Yes. I'm not sure that there's any point, anyhow."

The judgment felt like another blow, which she absorbed in silence while he drove.

Don't let it show, Alicia. Keep it all in.

Faking it.

Again.

"Tyler's annoying me," Abby announced from the backseat.

She took a breath, put some energy into her voice. "What's he doing, honey?"

"He's just annoying me."

Alicia craned around to look, but there was no annoying behavior in evidence.

"He's *breathing too much,*" Abby clarified.

"Well, I think you can put up with that for another couple of minutes."

The hour until they needed to leave for the reception dinner passed in child-oriented triviality. Alicia and MJ could have managed to talk some more if he had given the slightest signal that he wanted to, but he didn't.

She didn't know if his stubbornness and anger came from inner pain or wounded pride. He probably didn't know, either. Couples had divorced for less. Maybe they still had a chance at saving something if only they could talk, if only they could keep trying, but if MJ never allowed the talking to happen, and if he didn't want to try anymore, they were sunk. She didn't see a way out.

They were among the last to arrive at the restaurant, finding their names on folded pieces of card at one of two long tables set out in a back room reserved for private functions. It was a warm, elegant room with long windows looking out onto a night garden made dramatic and beautiful by hidden lighting.

She and MJ had been placed at the family table beside Claudia's father and stepmother, with Abby next to Daddy and Tyler in a high chair at the end. The other table was mainly reserved for friends, with Scarlett and Daniel also seated there, and after the cocktail hour that Alicia and MJ had skipped, the ice was already broken between most of the guests who hadn't met before.

How am I going to get through this?

But she did, of course. She'd had plenty of practice.

She made courteous conversation with Len and Dorie Schmidt, kept the children as well-mannered and quiet as she could, took a turn of holding Ben and then handed him back to Claudia to be fed. He fell asleep in his mommy's arms, and at a wedding like this, that seemed the right thing to happen. Everyone ate seafood and duck and filet steak, and talked and laughed. Nobody minded when Abby and Tyler got a little restless and ran around to visit Grandma and Grandpa, and Aunt Scarlett and new uncle Dan.

"Because this wedding is not just about us," Andy said, when he stood to make a short speech, thanking everyone—for being great parents, siblings and friends, for making the journey, for the gifts. "And finally, thanks to my beautiful sister-in-law, Alicia, for the fabulous cake she made for us, which we're going to cut as soon as the staff bring it in."

"Hold on a second, Andy." Michael wanted to say a few words, as well. He stood a little unsteadily.

He didn't normally drink very much, just a glass or two of wine, but Alicia thought he'd had more than that tonight—a refill on his gin and tonic earlier, and both white and red wine with the sumptuous meal.

It was his son's wedding, after all, and a first for the McKinley family, since none of them had been in Las Vegas to attend Alicia and MJ's. Michael could be a difficult man sometimes, his intelligence and capability and pride translating into impatience and overly high expectations. Andy and Scarlett had both felt the pressure of those expectations, and MJ had only escaped them because his expectations of himself had been equally high.

"It's a huge pleasure to be here tonight with all of you," Michael began.

The two tables went quiet, and Helen craned to look up at him, which was difficult from where she sat at his side. He rubbed his breastbone for a moment, as if the rich, delicious food was giving him trouble, and launched into a speech that Alicia suspected might go on a little too long if Helen didn't manage to give him a stern eye.

He told a joke about Andy in his teens, and the "What if I'm pregnant?" question hit Alicia again for no reason at that moment—it was on her mind more and more as each hour passed—so that she missed the punch line and couldn't laugh along with everyone else, while Michael waited for the room to go quiet again. His face looked twisted and strained.

MJ stood up, for some reason. He moved slowly and rather cautiously away from his seat, as if he didn't want to call attention to his action, and his eyes were fixed on his father. Alicia didn't understand it. He was like a tiger stalking a kill, so focused, trying not to be seen. Everyone else settled after the laughter, but Michael didn't start speaking again; he just stood there, then lifted an uncertain hand to the left side of his jaw, while his right hand clawed across his chest and clutched his arm.

"But that was a long time ago," he finally said, with a massive effort at a smile, and with a sense of horror, Alicia understood what was happening—from MJ's lightning-fast reaction far more than from her father-in-law's face. She pulled her purse from where it hung from its strap on the back of her chair.

MJ reached his father just in time. "Dad! Dad!" He was swaying and his face was pale and gray. MJ caught him, wrapping his arms around him like a bear to support his weight. "Give us some space," he ordered. Michael had sagged against him, his face slack. "Dad, can you speak to me!"

But no words came.

"Michael…" came Helen's terrified voice.

Andy was the next to react, moving just seconds after his brother. "Is it his heart?"

"Has to be. But I won't rule out something else until I'm sure."

Andy began to push the chairs aside, to give MJ enough space on the floor. Michael was lying there now, flat on his back and ominously still. "Call 911," MJ said. "Alicia!"

He didn't look at her, just flung her name into the room with the automatic assumption that she would be there because he needed her, that she would be ready to listen and respond, and she told him quickly, "Yes, I am. I'm calling." She'd already found the phone in her tiny evening bag, thankful that little else was in there. At the periphery of her vision she saw other people with their phones, putting them away as soon as she signaled that she'd got through.

"What is your emergency?" The dispatcher's voice was tinny and distant, but the whole room had gone quiet now, so she had no trouble hearing.

Quiet except for Abby's little voice suddenly. "What's happened to Grandpa?" Dorie stepped in to answer her, and Alicia kept her focus on the phone.

"My father-in-law is having a heart attack. We need an ambulance."

"Here, Alicia, beside me," MJ said. "I need to relay—" He didn't take the time to finish. He was already pulling at his father's formal wedding clothing—the tailored suit and buttoned shirt, the stiff collar and tie. She reached his side a moment later. He felt for a pulse, checked for breathing, made sure there was an adequate airway, all in the space of seconds. His surgeon's hands moved with instinct and precision, and his focus was total. "Tell them it's serious. We have doctors present. I'm about to start CPR."

She relayed all this while MJ made the first series of compressions, with a force that would have frightened her if she hadn't trusted absolutely that he knew what he was doing.

"Scarlett, defibrillator, can you check?" he barked out. "Some restaurants have them."

Helen was gasping in her seat, struggling to find the strength to move. A nurse until her marriage and a wife or mother to four doctors, she would have all the worst scenarios playing out in her head.

"Can I take that, Alicia?" Andy said, appearing in front of her with his hand held out for the phone.

She handed it over, understanding at once that with his medical training it made sense for him to take over, and he spoke into it, giving details to the dispatcher about Michael's age and medical history that she hadn't fully known. MJ paused in his work and gave two slow breaths, but Michael still wasn't responding. MJ began the compressions again, counting under his breath and using his full body weight.

Scarlett had briefly left the room but came back to report on the defibrillator. "They don't have one."

Alicia turned to Helen, who wanted to move to her husband's side but couldn't, because the strength in her legs had failed. They put their arms around each other, and Helen said feebly, "Thank you, Alicia dear... Just... help me up?"

"I'm here. Hold on to me as much as you need."

Helen was shaking. Together they crept to Michael's side, and Alicia helped her mother-in-law drop to the floor to take his hand. MJ was still pumping his father's chest, pausing every thirty counts for those slow breaths. He muttered something about the lack of equipment and medication.

"Ambulance should be ten minutes or less," Andy reported.

"Which hospital?" MJ asked, the words thumping out in time to the rhythm of his hands. "Mitchum?"

"Spring Ridge."

"It's farther."

"Five minutes. We're almost midway between the two, here. Spring Ridge is better for cardiac stuff."

"Yes, MJ, Andy's right," Scarlett said. "It's a bigger

hospital. We should push for Spring Ridge, if there's any question."

"Okay. Makes sense. Clear everyone out," MJ ordered. "I'm sorry, Andy, Claudia. Your wedding."

"No one's thinking about that," Andy said. "You're right. We need people to leave."

"Not me," Helen said. "Oh, Michael, Michael!" She was too terrified to cry, and if anyone in the family doubted that she and Michael still loved each other after their thirty-eight years of marriage, the doubt was gone now.

"Mom, are you sure...?" Andy said.

"I'm not leaving him. I'm going in the ambulance. He's not speaking. He's not responding. Oh, Michael, don't you do this!" She controlled a sob of fear. "I'm here. I'm right here with you."

MJ said nothing, just kept up with his chest compressions, his face set and intent with effort as he counted compressions and breaths.

"Let me take over, MJ," Andy said.

"No. Not yet. If I have to."

No one wanted to get in the way. Scarlett was white-faced, with a worried Daniel shadowing her side. Abby had begun to cry. Giving Helen's free hand a final squeeze, Alicia left her and went to reassure the children. The restaurant staff understood the challenging situation and offered another function room—upstairs and unoccupied tonight—for everyone to use.

The guests got themselves up there, but then Andy, Claudia and Scarlett put their heads together and told everyone to go, making the kind of automatic apologies and thanks that meant nothing and everything, and that no one took in. By the time the ambulance arrived, some people had already left, while others—Helen's sister and her husband, Claudia's father and his wife—still stood in awkward couples and groupings.

The paramedics took over where MJ left off, complete with medication and the defibrillator they'd been desperate for, and there was a notable shift in the tension when it became apparent they'd had some success. They started making preparations to take him to hospital.

We never had the cake. I worked so hard on it, and then this happened.

It was the kind of odd, left-field thought that seemed to pop out of nowhere at a time like this. Alicia felt almost numb, and all she could do was keep the children happy and answer Abby's anxious questions. After what seemed a very long time, the paramedics finished the preparations and wheeled Michael away to the ambulance. "You're not going with them?" Alicia asked MJ. She wanted to take his arm, or lean into him, some kind of body contact, but didn't know if he'd push her away.

"Crowded enough with Mom," he said. "We'll follow."

"Yes."

"If they can get him stable tonight…" He paused and looked at her as if seeing her for the first time. "I'm sorry. The children will be exhausted. Take them home, if you want."

"No. If they fall asleep in our laps in the waiting room, it doesn't matter."

She wanted to be with him. She didn't know if it meant anything that he had turned first to her, out of all the people present, when he'd needed someone to call 911. Maybe it was pure habit. But she couldn't leave him, not when she could see the fear in his face. He and his father were close…similar…they shared a name. He would be devastated—would blame himself—if the worst happened. She needed to be with him.

He swore suddenly. "This is Andy and Claudia's wedding night. They were supposed to be leaving Ben with her dad and Dorie. They had that luxury hotel booked in Warren for a night on their own."

"They're taking Ben home," Alicia told him. "They're going to wait there for news. The last thing they're going to feel is disappointment at a time like this. They'll have their wedding night and their honeymoon another time."

He was still frowning, barely seeing her. "And Scarlett and Dan?"

"Going to Spring Ridge."

"All the guests…"

"They understand, MJ. Most of them have left. People understand."

He squeezed her hand and again she didn't know what it meant. He dropped the contact before she could squeeze back, but it probably wasn't deliberate. His focus was vague and shifting, and she knew he was tortured by whether he'd done enough for his father—whether his CPR had been effective, whether the ambulance had gotten here soon enough, whether the medication and treatment would work or if too much damage to the heart had already been done.

"You did all you could."

"He was breathing. His pulse was there. He was showing a response to the medication and oxygen." MJ was talking to himself. She ran her hand down his arm, felt his warmth and scent and strength so close but still so far out of reach.

They strapped Abby and Tyler into their seats and Alicia drove. MJ didn't question it until they pulled into the hospital parking lot twenty minutes later, when he simply said, "Thanks for—" and didn't finish the sentence, as he looked down almost in surprise at the passenger door he was about to close, as if he'd only just realized he wasn't in the driver's seat.

Chapter Seventeen

They waited for three hours—a tedious blur of vending-machine coffee and meaningless reassurances to each other.

Abby fell asleep in MJ's lap, while Alicia kept Tyler hugged close in her own arms. Her spine ached from holding him in the uncomfortable waiting-room chair but she didn't begrudge the pain and discomfort because his little body gave her an anchor to hope and connected her to MJ, who was seated beside her with his shoulder pressed against hers.

Our kids.

Am I pregnant?

Ours.

Protecting them in their sleep, while we wait for news of their grandfather.

Finally it came.

When he saw the doctor enter the waiting area, MJ

quickly eased Abby onto the chair and Alicia took the weight of her head against her shoulder. Abby stirred and mumbled but stayed asleep, while MJ strode to meet the doctor, along with Scarlett and Helen. They stayed in a huddle with the man for several minutes, in a little alcove that only just kept them in sight, and Alicia could only crane her head over Tyler's to try to read their body language.

Good.

The news was good. She could tell from MJ's face as soon as he turned to come back to her. The way he walked revealed it, also. There was a new energy and a palpable relief. "He's stable and conscious. He's spoken. They think he'll be all right now, even though it might be a long road."

"Oh, that's wonderful!" Tears of relief flooded her eyes.

"Mom is going to stay. I'm not sure that she should, but she's refusing to consider any other option. We'll get the kids home."

"She'll need some things, and so will your father. I'll pack a bag for them tonight."

Helen was coming toward them and heard this offer from Alicia. "Would you, Alicia dear? That would be wonderful!" Her voice shook. "Don't pack it tonight, though. You must be exhausted. Bring it in the morning. Can I give you a list? Oh, but what to put on it?" She worked her hands together, unable to focus. She looked very tired and wrung out, inappropriately well-dressed in her sage-green mother-of-the-groom dress and matching jacket, lipstick worn away.

"Let me pack everything I think of," Alicia reassured her, "and I'll call you in case there's anything you want to add."

"Yes, of course," Helen said. "Yes, that's the best plan, isn't it?"

"Go up to him, Mom," MJ told her, with a hand on her arm.

"Unit 5A?"

"Yes, that's right."

"So that'll be the fifth floor?"

"Yes, and make a left out of the elevator."

"I'll go up with her," Scarlett said. "And I'll call Andy, let him know how Dad is. He said he wanted the news as soon as we had it. Get those kids home, guys, and we'll see you in the morning." She and Helen headed toward the elevator.

"Can you manage Tyler, if I carry Abby?" MJ said to Alicia.

"I'm fine. He's not that heavy."

They drove home, too tired to do more than talk briefly about Michael's condition. The children woke up just enough to make a bathroom visit and cooperate with Alicia's efforts in getting them into their pajamas, and Tyler into the diaper he still needed at night. They were asleep again moments after she tucked them in. It was after three in the morning.

She found MJ in the bedroom, staring helplessly at the bed his parents had slept in the night before. "I don't know where we should sleep. I don't think I'll be able to, in any case." It sounded as if he was talking about them sharing a bed, but then he seemed to remember.

They didn't need to fake their marriage now that his parents weren't here.

"Look," he continued, much more stiffly, "why don't you take the sofa bed, and I'll sleep here?"

"All right." She tried to keep the emotion out of her voice.

Am I pregnant? My period was due today, but it hasn't

come. What will he do when I tell him that? Will I tell him,
or will I wait until I know for sure?

After she went downstairs, she could faintly hear him
in the upstairs corridor, going along to the bathroom and
back, closing the bedroom door. If it had meant anything
that he'd called on her in the first frantic minutes of his
father's heart attack, he seemed to be turning his back
on it now.

Morning came after a short and restless night's sleep.
The children woke up with the morning light the way
they usually did, although Alicia was sure they would
both need long naps today. She made breakfast for them,
listening for evidence that MJ was up, too, but the first
thing she heard was the front door opening. He was going
for a run.

She followed him to find him stretching in the front
yard. "I couldn't sleep," he said as soon as he saw her. "I
need to get out. I called the hospital—"

"Oh, you did?"

"Upstairs, on my cell. Dad had a good night. Mom is
holding up."

"I'll pack that bag for her, as soon as I've fed the kids."

"Thanks." He straightened, cutting short his warm-up
as a way of ending their interaction. The connection she'd
been so desperate to believe in last night had gone. "Andy
and Claudia left for the hospital a half hour ago. I don't
know if you heard them," he said.

"No, I didn't. I was probably in the shower."

"Right, I guess you were. I'm off."

"Okay." She stood on the porch and watched him as he
disappeared down the street, his need to avoid her sting-
ing in her chest like a knife.

While Abby and Tyler ate their breakfast, she put together everything she thought Helen and Michael would need, then parked the kids in front of the electronic baby-sitter, aka a DVD, and called Helen to run through the list.

"Alicia, this is wonderful," Helen said in a shaky voice. "You've thought of everything."

"We'll bring it to the hospital as soon as we can," she promised, hiding behind the kind of marital "we" that no one questioned, and indeed Helen didn't ask if it would be her or MJ or the whole family.

"Thank you so much. I—I appreciate you in so many ways, Alicia dear. I don't think I tell you that enough. Something like this…has made me realize. As much as it makes me realize how I love Michael. I should say it. We should all say it. Far more often than we do. How much we care about each other."

"Yes, we should," she said with difficulty. "You're right. We should say it. I care about you, too, Helen. I really do. And about Michael. I'm sending all our love to both of you, and we'll see you soon."

"Yes, all right. I need to get back to him. Later, then. Goodbye."

MJ still hadn't returned from his run. She checked on the kids, who were still happy with Disney, then she popped into the bathroom, and—

She wasn't pregnant.

Right on cue, maybe half a day late, the evidence had come. Numbly, she opened a new pack of tampons and dealt with the situation, hardly recognizing her own reflection in the mirror as she washed her hands.

Yes, this was Alicia. Nonpregnant Alicia. Same as ever. Pale and tired and unsmiling, drying her hands on a fluffy towel for far longer than necessary, because her last little jewel of hope had just fallen through her fingers and she had no idea how to pick up her life from here.

She felt the first sob rise up in her throat and didn't try to hold it back.

MJ needed to turn here and return to the house. He'd been out running for too long, but he didn't want to go back, because that meant confronting all the people he didn't want to face.

His children, who didn't yet know—and wouldn't really understand when they did—that they were about to be plunged into the ongoing consequences of a divorce.

His wife, who'd walked out on him, strung him along with an apparent willingness to reconsider and then admitted under his point-blank questioning that she hadn't married him for *himself* but for the material trappings, as he'd always known in his heart.

Worse, she had destroyed his naive illusion that she'd quickly fallen in love with him after their wedding—on their wedding night, even—and had done everything for the best and most honest of reasons from then on. That was the kicker. That was the crunch. That she'd kept up the pretense for so long.

Finally, he didn't want to face his parents and siblings, who'd never really taken Alicia into their hearts and who would be unhappy but not surprised about the announcement he would soon need to make. It seemed ironic that he hadn't wanted to spoil Andy and Claudia's wedding with the cloud of an impending divorce, and now Dad had spoiled it with something equally devastating.

But at least Dad was going to be okay.

MJ knew that he and Alicia weren't. He felt like a fool for not realizing that their connection wasn't real. What kind of a world had he been living in these past seven years? It was his fault, too. He accepted that. She was right. He was *never there.* But the loss of face was intense.

Intense, and dwarfed by the gut-wrenching loss of Alicia herself.

Hell, he didn't want to lose her!

Why had she said that she loved him, yesterday? Why then, when it was too late? It had come out of left field, in the middle of their talk about faking it at the wedding and about whether she needed professional help with the kids. He didn't know why she would have said it, what she hoped to gain from throwing out those loaded, meaningless words.

Loaded and meaningless.

That was a complete contradiction.

He didn't care. It was true.

His feet pounded the pavement with all of it echoing in his head. *I love you.* Loaded and meaningless. *I love you.* Real and fake.

The trouble with being married for seven years and having two kids together was that it all got so complicated. You could find evidence in their shared past for anything you wanted. That their marriage was doomed from the beginning. That they had a great partnership. That they'd married each other for the worst reasons. And for the best.

Only a few hundred yards to the house now. He could see it looming behind the trees that lined the street. He didn't know what he would find when he went inside. Out of breath, since he'd run hard and spent more energy than during his usual gym visit, he walked around on the front lawn for several minutes to cool down, then grabbed the hand towel he'd flung onto the porch swing and wiped the worst of the sweat from his neck and forehead. He could hear a Disney movie playing inside.

And he could see the Disney movie, and the kids content in front of it, when he came into the front hall.

But he couldn't see Alicia.

She wasn't with the children or in the kitchen or the laundry room. Upstairs, she wasn't packing the overnight bag for Mom, because there it sat on the bed, filled and zippered.

She was in the bathroom. He heard the faucets gushing and then cutting off, and decided to head back downstairs so that they wouldn't be caught together in this narrow corridor with nothing good left to say to each other.

But the bathroom door opened before he could move, and there she was.

There she was. Face blotchy and red. Eyes and nose swollen. No makeup. Hair damp around her forehead from where she'd clearly been splashing her face with cold water in a vain effort to hide the evidence of the tears.

He thought of Dad at once, and his legs lost their strength. He stepped forward, unsteady. "What's wrong? Did they call from the hospital? What's happened to him?"

She shook her head. "He's fine. They haven't called."

"Then what?"

"It's nothing. It's fine."

"It is not damn well fine, Alicia!" His hair-trigger emotions switched track like a runaway train. "You've been crying. For minutes. It is not fine. Do not fake your feelings *now,* when my father is in the hospital and we're getting a divorce and you've been faking so much for seven years!"

"I'm not pregnant," she said. Her shoulders were high and tense and she had her arms folded over her stomach. "That's all."

"You're not pregnant? Did you…? Were you…?" He wasn't getting this. He just…wasn't getting it.

And suddenly he didn't care that he wasn't getting it, and he just wanted to hold her, the way he always did. The way he always had, from that moment in that tacky street-corner restaurant in Manhattan when she'd said to him that his work was more important than hers, with such sincerity and appreciation, and he'd felt the bright hint of a connection.

She hadn't faked that.

"I thought I might have been," she said thinly. "Remember that night in the kitchen?"

"Of course I remember it. We were—" *Incandescent together.*

"The timing was right." Her voice was even thinner. "But I'm not."

"Hell!" he said, because everything was hell right now, and took her into his arms before either of them had time to question anything.

"I know," she sobbed. "I wanted it so much." She thought he'd sworn because there wasn't going to be a baby. And maybe he had. "I thought it was the only chance we had left, the only reason I could think of that might make you want to keep trying, like I do, and now it's gone."

He let her cry and just held her, craving the familiar feel and smell and warmth of her, wanting to heal everything with his touch and his presence, feeling the hard lump in his own throat and sharing her sense of loss. She wasn't pretending about this. No one could cry like this if it wasn't real. No woman could hold and cling to a man like this if she didn't care.

He didn't know what it all meant just yet. He didn't know what it might make possible. He didn't want to think about partnerships or false assumptions or changed feelings or anything. He just wanted to hold her and stay in this moment, with her body pressed into his and his arms trying to soothe away the jerking rhythm of her sobs.

He kissed the top of her head, where the blond strands came in more colors than he could count, wheat and honey and white light and who knew what else. He kissed her wet lashes and swollen lids. He kissed her trembling mouth and warm cheeks. He kissed her fragrant neck. He squeezed her so hard that his body shook, because the fierceness of what he felt had nowhere to go.

"Alicia, I love you so much," he whispered, before he even knew the words were going to come.

"I love you. I *love* you, MJ. I've done so many things wrong. I know that...."

"So have I. I've done a million wrong things. I've taken our marriage for granted, set it in stone, based it on my agenda alone, never realized that it needed to change and grow."

"...but only because I was trying to do them perfectly."

He realized that she was blaming herself and barely taking in his own confession. "That's not possible. Listen! It's not possible to be perfect, and I'm not asking you to. Please don't."

"I thought it was all I had to offer. My looks. My support at home."

"Be *you*. I love *you*."

"But you think you don't know me. You think I've faked everything."

"I'm wrong about that. When I really think. When I think back. Fearing I'd lose you has made me think back a lot."

"Me, too. So much."

"I accused you of it because I was so angry and scared. I wanted to make you admit to the worst of it. I was terrified that I'd never known you at all."

"I'm sorry."

"I married you because I saw through to who you were. Because of those secondhand dresses that you managed to carry off like designer gowns. Because of the times you couldn't hide that you were scared. Because of your kindness."

"My kindness?"

"You're a kind person, Alicia. You couldn't fake that. You're good to Mom. You never bad-mouth people behind their backs. You would never, ever behave like Anna with James over their daughter." His throat tightened again and he was so close to tears that he felt them welling and threatening to spill. "And you couldn't fake crying like this, either."

She laughed. Shakily. "No, I really couldn't."

He was laughing, too. "Hey, did you hear what I just did?"

"What?"

"The three-things game. I just told you three things I love about you. The way you could wear a secondhand dress, the way you were scared and your kindness."

"Want me to play it, too?"

Did he? He laughed again. "Yes, please."

She thought for a moment. "Your intelligence, your sense of honor and the way you're clueless sometimes."

"You love me because I'm clueless?"

"About some things. Like how to get the kids out of the bath without having them cry. Like whether something's home-cooked or catered-in or bought from the store. It's cute. Oh, and I love you because you can't cope with being bored. And because you like bracing cold air. And because the smell of you makes me melt. And because you're a great doctor. And because you'd never do anything that would hurt the kids. And because you're proud of being like your dad."

"We are way beyond three things now."

"You want me to stop?"

"I don't want any of this to stop. Alicia, I don't want our marriage to stop. I *don't*. Ever."

"No?" she whispered. She laid her head against his chest, as if she wanted to feel the beat of his heart.

"No," he said scratchily. "That's the kicker. I love you, and I thought you knew that even when I didn't say it. I thought you felt it growing in both of us, the way I felt it, and if you're saying all of the really important stuff is real— I know you are saying that."

"I am. Oh, I am. It couldn't hurt this much if it wasn't real, MJ."

"Hell, it makes all the difference! I love you. All it has to be is real, and then it's perfect."

"I love you so much. I didn't even know it, because the anger grew at the same time, but when I realized, I knew I had to be honest, and that backfired and—"

"Didn't backfire. We had to say it and feel it. All of it. I love that you're my wife. I'm intensely proud of you. It killed me to believe you'd faked our whole marriage. And I understand why you felt you had to leave." He took a deep breath. Was it still too soon? She'd asked that they take some time over this. Surely it wasn't still too soon! "Will you come back, Alicia, darling, sweetheart, beautiful wife?"

"Yes. Oh, yes."

"And will you tell me any time something's not right? If you have an ambition that's unfulfilled or a need that's not met? If you want another baby."

"Oh, I do! I would love another one. You always said three or four."

"If you want to study or train for something when the kids are older?"

"I'd like that. I've been thinking about studying catering and kitchen management and opening a business. That's years away."

"It is, but I'd support you in it, all the way. We can think about it. Talk about it. Do it right."

"Maybe we should concentrate on getting me pregnant, first."

"I think we should definitely concentrate on that," he whispered. "We'd better be prepared to work quite hard at it...."

"Very, very hard."

"With lots of preparation and warm-up."

"Warm-up?"

"Can I kiss you, please? To get in some practice?"

"Kiss me quickly, because we don't have much time."

"Only the rest of our lives," he whispered and bent his head to find her mouth.

Chapter Eighteen

Seven months later...

"I never pegged you for the big-society-wedding type, sis," said MJ to Scarlett. Alicia sat beside him, her arms bare and cool in the summer air-conditioning and a softly draped blue-gray silk dress light and floaty against her skin.

"Well, *someone* in the family had to do it this way," Scarlett answered.

She surveyed the luxurious Manhattan ballroom where their wedding reception was being held. The main course of their sit-down dinner had just been served, and at the bridal table, the mood was lighthearted and relaxed. "Or I think Mom's heart would have broken."

"After your wedding in Las Vegas," she continued, "when we didn't find out until after the fact that you'd actually done it. And then when Andy and Claudia's was shadowed by Dad's heart attack." Michael was fully recovered now and had made some important lifestyle changes, including bringing forward his retirement and planned trip to Europe with Helen by nearly two years. "Daniel's and mine was the only one left," Scarlett concluded. She smiled out at the crowded function room, looking serenely content about the way her wedding plans had changed, her gaze automatically drawn to Daniel, who'd briefly left the table to request a particular song from the band.

"That's a very negative way of looking at the situation," MJ said sternly. "There's always divorce. That brings the possibility of remarriage and a big wedding into the picture very nicely."

"Divorce!" Scarlett said scathingly.

"Not so impossible, is it?"

"With Andy and Claudia expecting a baby in October and still acting like newlyweds? And Daniel and me with the ink on our marriage certificate barely dry? I don't think so!" She glanced sideways, and her smile brought Alicia closer into the conversation. "As for you two, there were a couple of times…" She frowned. "I'll be honest, MJ—" she leaned onto the table a little, the beaded accent at the empire waist of her champagne-colored satin gown catching the light and her V neckline fluid and oh, so pretty against her skin "—when I thought you two might have been headed for an ugly split…" She looked at them, tilted her head to one side and frowned.

Alicia blushed.

"But now," Scarlett continued, "I'd put you as the most rock solid of the lot of us, including Mom and Dad, and they've been together almost forty years."

"Oh, you would?" MJ said. Beneath the table, Alicia felt his hand slide over hers, against her thigh. They both squeezed, as if to say that they agreed completely with

Scarlett's assessment. That didn't mean they planned to let her get away without an explanation. "Where's your evidence?" he demanded.

"Think about it," Scarlett said. "More than seven years in, two gorgeous kids, just back from a Florida vacation with big smiles on your faces, another baby on the way."

Alicia smiled at this. After the way she'd sobbed in MJ's arms about not being accidentally pregnant last October, they'd quickly firmed their emotional decision that baby number three would be very much wanted and planned. She'd conceived the following month and was due in August, three and a half months from now, and they'd chosen not to find out if it would be a brother for Tyler or a sister for Abby.

Seated a couple of seats farther down, Andy had tuned in to the conversation now. "It's not their mileage or their productivity, Scarlett," he said. "It's their glow."

"Their glow?"

"I guess you've been too busy planning this bride fest to notice. They've been glowing for, oh, about seven months now."

"Hmm, looking back," Scarlett said thoughtfully, "you might be right."

"I know I'm right. You say that Claudia and I still look like newlyweds, but I think MJ and Alicia could give us a run for our money."

"Oh, you're not going to go all McKinley competitive on us, the two of you, and start vying for which is the happiest brother in the family!" Scarlett scoffed. "Honestly, I thank my lucky stars I'm a girl!"

"There's no competition," Andy said smugly. "Because this is one we can all win."

"Who's talking about winning?" Michael said. He'd

been circulating through the room and had just appeared at the bridal table.

"We're talking about being happy."

"I heard the word *win* in there somewhere. I know I did."

"Okay, Dad," Andy admitted. "We were talking about which McKinley couple wins in the marital-happiness stakes. I said we could all be winners there."

"Well, I don't agree," Michael said, standing taller, the way he always did when there was a point to be proved. "I think there's no question that your mother and I win that one. Thirty-nine years and counting. How do you compete with that?"

Once again, MJ squeezed Alicia's hand—and her thigh—under the table. "Just give us time, Dad," he said, "I have every intention of competing with you and Mom in this, all the way."

* * * * *

COMING NEXT MONTH from Harlequin®
Special Edition®
AVAILABLE JULY 24, 2012

#2203 PUPPY LOVE IN THUNDER CANYON
Montana Mavericks: Back in the Saddle
Christyne Butler
An intense, aloof surgeon meets his match in a friendly librarian who believes that emotional connections can heal—and she soon teaches him that love is the best medicine!

#2204 THE DOCTOR AND THE SINGLE MOM
Men of Mercy Medical
Teresa Southwick
Dr. Adam Stone picked the wrong place to rent. Or maybe just the wrong lady to rent from. Jill Beck is beloved—and protected—by the entire town. One wrong move with the sexy single mom could cost him a career in Blackwater Lake, Montana—and the chance to fill up the empty place inside him.

#2205 RILEY'S BABY BOY
Reunion Brides
Karen Rose Smith
Feuding families make a surpise baby and even bigger challenges. Are Brenna McDougall and Riley O'Rourke ready for everything life has in store for them? Including a little surpise romance?

#2206 HIS BEST FRIEND'S WIFE
Gina Wilkins
How much is widowed mom Renae Sanchez willing to risk for a sexy, secretive man from her past...a man she once blamed for her husband's death?

#2207 A WEEK TILL THE WEDDING
Linda Winstead Jones
Jacob Tasker and Daisy Bell think they are doing the right thing when they pretend to still be engaged for the sake of his sick grandmother. But as their fake nuptials start leading to real love, they find out that granny may have a few tricks up her old sleeve!

#2208 ONE IN A BILLION
Home to Harbor Town
Beth Kery
A potential heiress—the secret baby of her mother's affair—is forced by the will to work with her nemesis, a sexy tycoon, to figure out the truth about her paternity, and what it means for the company of which she now owns half!

You can find more information on upcoming Harlequin® titles, free excerpts and more at www.HarlequinInsideRomance.com.   HSECNM0712

REQUEST YOUR FREE BOOKS!

2 FREE NOVELS PLUS 2 FREE GIFTS!

⑤ Harlequin®

SPECIAL EDITION

Life, Love & Family

YES! Please send me 2 FREE Harlequin® Special Edition novels and my 2 FREE gifts (gifts are worth about $10). After receiving them, if I don't wish to receive any more books, I can return the shipping statement marked "cancel." If I don't cancel, I will receive 6 brand-new novels every month and be billed just $4.49 per book in the U.S. or $5.24 per book in Canada. That's a saving of at least 14% off the cover price! It's quite a bargain! Shipping and handling is just 50¢ per book in the U.S. and 75¢ per book in Canada.* I understand that accepting the 2 free books and gifts places me under no obligation to buy anything. I can always return a shipment and cancel at any time. Even if I never buy another book, the two free books and gifts are mine to keep forever.

235/335 HDN FEGF

Name	(PLEASE PRINT)
Address	Apt. #
City	State/Prov.	Zip/Postal Code

Signature (if under 18, a parent or guardian must sign)

Mail to the **Reader Service:**
IN U.S.A.: P.O. Box 1867, Buffalo, NY 14240-1867
IN CANADA: P.O. Box 609, Fort Erie, Ontario L2A 5X3

Not valid for current subscribers to Harlequin Special Edition books.

Want to try two free books from another line?
Call 1-800-873-8635 or visit www.ReaderService.com.

* Terms and prices subject to change without notice. Prices do not include applicable taxes. Sales tax applicable in N.Y. Canadian residents will be charged applicable taxes. Offer not valid in Quebec. This offer is limited to one order per household. All orders subject to credit approval. Credit or debit balances in a customer's account(s) may be offset by any other outstanding balance owed by or to the customer. Please allow 4 to 6 weeks for delivery. Offer available while quantities last.

Your Privacy—The Reader Service is committed to protecting your privacy. Our Privacy Policy is available online at www.ReaderService.com or upon request from the Reader Service.

We make a portion of our mailing list available to reputable third parties that offer products we believe may interest you. If you prefer that we not exchange your name with third parties, or if you wish to clarify or modify your communication preferences, please visit us at www.ReaderService.com/consumerchoice or write to us at Reader Service Preference Service, P.O. Box 9062, Buffalo, NY 14269. Include your complete name and address.

HSE11B

Harlequin® *Super Romance®*

*Enjoy a month of compelling, emotional stories, including
a poignant new tale of love lost and found from*

Sarah Mayberry

When Angela Bartlett loses her best friend to a rare heart
condition, it seems only natural that she step in and help
widower and friend Michael Young. The last thing she
expects is to find herself falling for him....

Within Reach

Available August 7!

HARLEQUIN®
RECOMMENDED
Read!

Find more great stories this month from
Harlequin® Superromance® at

www.Harlequin.com

HSRSM71795

Angie Bartlett and Michael Robinson are friends. And following the death of his wife, Angie's best friend, their bond has grown even more. But that's all there is…right?

Read on for an exciting excerpt of WITHIN REACH by Sarah Mayberry, available August 2012 from Harlequin® Superromance®.

"HEY. RIGHT ON TIME," Michael said as he opened the door.

The first thing Angie registered was his fresh haircut and that he was clean shaven—a significant change from the last time she'd visited. Then her gaze dropped to his broad chest and the skintight black running pants molded to his muscular legs. The words died on her lips and she blinked, momentarily stunned by her acute awareness of him.

"You've cut your hair," she said stupidly.

"Yeah. Decided it was time to stop doing my caveman impersonation."

He gestured for her to enter. As she brushed past him she caught the scent of his spicy deodorant. He preceded her to the kitchen and her gaze traveled across his shoulders before dropping to his backside. Angie had always made a point of not noticing Michael's body. They were friends and she didn't want to know that kind of stuff. Now, however, she was forcibly reminded that he was a *very* attractive man.

Suddenly she didn't know where to look.

It was then that she noticed the other changes—the clean kitchen, the polished dining table and the living room free of clutter and abandoned clothes.

"Look at you go." Surely these efforts meant he was rejoining life.

He shrugged, but seemed pleased she'd noticed. "Getting there."

They maintained eye contact and the moment expanded. A connection that went beyond the boundaries of their friendship formed between them. Suddenly Angie wanted Michael in ways she'd never felt before. *Ever.*

"Okay. Let's get this show on the road," his six-year-old daughter, Eva, announced as she marched into the room.

Angie shook her head to break the spell and focused on Eva. "Great. Looking forward to a little light shopping?"

"Yes!" Eva gave a squeal of delight, then kissed her father goodbye.

Angie didn't feel 100 percent comfortable until she was sliding into the driver's seat.

Which was dumb. It was nothing. A stupid, odd bit of awareness that meant *nothing.* Michael was still Michael, even if he was gorgeous. Just because she'd tuned in to that fact for a few seconds didn't change anything.

Does Angie's new awareness mark a permanent shift in their relationship? Find out in WITHIN REACH by Sarah Mayberry, available August 2012 from Harlequin® Superromance®.